Maybe it was the way he was looking at her—maybe it was because she was tired—or maybe it was because she didn't want to be friends with this man.

She wanted only to think of him as Harry's father—her employers—she didn't want him to try and be her friend. It felt...dangerous. He made her thoughts fly in directions she didn't want them to go.

'I'm tired,' she said. 'If you don't mind, I think I'll turn in for the night.'

Suddenly his hand was in her hair, and he leant down and kissed her lightly on the lips. For a moment the world spun. 'Goodnight, then, Colleen. I'll see you in the morning.'

Dear Reader

I almost always write my Medical Romances from my personal experience as a nurse, and this one is no different.

When Harry is badly injured in a car accident his father, barrister Daniel Frobisher, is determined to do everything in his power to save the son he didn't know he had and barely knows. His research for the right person to help his son leads him to sparky nurse Colleen McCulloch.

Following an accident that left her brother brain-injured, Colleen has made it her mission to make sure every patient under her care is given the best possible chance to improve. So when she meets Harry, who has lost almost everyone he loves, how can she resist taking up Daniel's offer of a job? Particularly when it gives her time away from her disastrous love-life…

Soon sparks fly, and as Colleen begins to see the tortured and grieving man behind Daniel's cool façade, professional distance goes out of the window and she becomes involved with this small, hurt family. And if Daniel makes her feel something that no man has ever made her feel, doesn't she just have to find a way to deal with that too?

I hope you enjoy Colleen and Daniel's story.

Anne Fraser

THE FIREBRAND WHO UNLOCKED HIS HEART

BY
ANNE FRASER

First published in Great Britain 2012
by Mills & Boon, an imprint of Harlequin (UK) Limited.
Harlequin (UK) Limited, Eton House, 18-24 Paradise Road,
Richmond, Surrey TW9 1SR

© Anne Fraser 2012

ISBN: 978 0 263 22865 6

Harlequin (UK) policy is to use papers that are natural, renewable and recyclable products and made from wood grown in sustainable forests. The logging and manufacturing process conform to the legal environmental regulations of the country of origin.

Printed and bound in Great Britain
by CPI Antony Rowe, Chippenham, Wiltshire

Anne Fraser was born in Scotland, but brought up in South Africa. After she left school she returned to the birthplace of her parents, the remote Western Islands of Scotland. She left there to train as a nurse, before going on to university to study English Literature. After the birth of her first child she and her doctor husband travelled the world, working in rural Africa, Australia and Northern Canada. Anne still works in the health sector. To relax, she enjoys spending time with her family, reading, walking and travelling.

Recent titles by the same author:

MISTLETOE, MIDWIFE…MIRACLE BABY
DOCTOR ON THE RED CARPET
THE PLAYBOY OF HARLEY STREET
THE DOCTOR AND THE DEBUTANTE
DAREDEVIL, DOCTOR…DAD!†
MIRACLE: MARRIAGE REUNITED
SPANISH DOCTOR, PREGNANT MIDWIFE*

The Brides of Penhally Bay
†*St Piran's Hospital*

These books are also available in eBook format from www.millsandboon.co.uk

For my wonderful and thankfully healthy daughters,
Rachel and Katherine.
You inspire me.

CHAPTER ONE

'I'M SORRY, but the answer is still no,' Colleen said.

Daniel Frobisher leaned back in his chair and wiped an imaginary fleck of dust from his dark-grey suit. He narrowed his eyes at her as if he couldn't believe what he was hearing.

He looks like a tiger studying his prey just before it attacks, Colleen thought. He was in his late thirties, she guessed, with light brown hair and intense green eyes. He had the kind of face that you wanted to stare at as if it were a painting. Long, straight nose, full mouth and cheekbones most models would give their designer gowns for. He was almost too good-looking. Men who looked like him were too *unreal* somehow.

'I'll pay you well. Very well,' he said in his Oxbridge accent and then went on to name a weekly sum that made Colleen's head reel. What he was proposing was more than she earned in a month. More than she earned in two months, come to think of it, but money wasn't the issue here.

'I don't need the money; besides I'm perfectly happy with my life the way it is,' Colleen said firmly. The last part wasn't exactly true, but there was no need for the man in front of her to know that.

This wasn't the first time she had said no. She had

told Daniel Frobisher's assistant—what was his name again? Haversham or something—the same thing over the phone only a few days ago.

'If Mr Frobisher can't spare the time to come and see me for himself, I'm afraid that tells me that he is not committed to making his son better,' Colleen had told Haversham. 'In order to make the greatest improvement, his son is going to need round-the-clock, intensive treatment. That means his father helping. A lot. And if he can't spare the time to meet me...' Colleen paused '...it's a non-starter.'

'Mr Frobisher is a very busy man,' Haversham replied. 'He would have come personally if he could have. He asked me to represent him in this matter.'

This matter? It was Frobisher's *son* they were talking about.

'Look, please tell him I'm sorry about his son, really I am. But if Mr Frobisher is as wealthy as you say he is, there are other arrangements he could make that would work better for him.'

She had said a polite goodbye, and forgotten all about it until this morning, when Daniel Frobisher himself had appeared, demanding to see her.

'There is a gorgeous-looking man asking to see you,' Lillian, the receptionist, had said, having come to find Colleen in the staff room where Colleen was giving her report to the on-coming staff before leaving for the day. 'I told him you were busy, but he says he needs to speak to you—right now.' Lillian's eyes had been round. 'You've been keeping him a secret from us, you naughty thing, although I can quite understand why. If I was two-timing my boyfriend—especially with someone who looks like that—I don't think I'd be telling anyone either.'

'I'm not two-timing Ciaran with anyone,' Colleen had protested. 'How can you even suggest such a thing? Tell whoever it is that he'll have to wait—or to come back on Monday.'

'Honey, whatever you've been up to with that man, he's not going anywhere.'

Mystified, Colleen had peeked around the corner. Lillian was right. Whoever he was, he was a hunk. Just because she was engaged to Ciaran didn't mean she couldn't recognise yumminess when she saw it. But the man pacing the floor, irritably checking his watch every couple of seconds, wasn't anyone she had met before. She would have remembered.

'I've never seen him before in my life. Did he give you a name?' Colleen had whispered to Lillian.

'Says he's called Mr Frobisher.'

So the too-busy man had come in person this time. Well, she'd be telling him exactly the same as she'd told Haversham. But he'd have to wait until she'd finished the handover to the night staff and changed out of her uniform.

After finishing the report, Colleen had gone to say goodbye to her patients, most of whom were getting ready for the day, either on their own or with help from the nursing staff. She had to use some fancy footwork to avoid being mowed down by Jake in his motorised wheelchair. 'Hey, Jake, you're not at Silverstone now,' she had chided affectionately. Jake was one of their longest residents on the rehab ward. When he'd come to them he'd been immobile and angry following a motorbike accident that had robbed him of the use of his legs. But since he'd been given the motorised chair, he'd become determined to be as independent as possible. He would be going home in a couple of weeks and she'd miss his cheeky grin.

Her last stop had been the room immediately opposite the nurse's station. Kiera Flannigan was an eighteen year old who had been involved in a serious road-traffic accident six months earlier that had left her paralysed from the neck down. Like Jake, she had initially refused to have anything to do with the rehab programme that had been devised for her. Colleen had spent hours by her bed, cajoling her, talking to her, refusing to let the teenager give up. And her efforts had paid off. Kiera was still paralysed—there was no hope of an improvement—but she was able to use a special computer that allowed her to use her breath to type on to a screen as well as guide her wheelchair around the ward.

'Hey, Colleen,' Kiera had typed. 'Are we going dancing tonight?'

'Too tired, Kiera. Need my beauty sleep,' Colleen had replied. 'What have you got planned for the day?'

'School work. Ugh,' Kiera had typed. 'Exams soon. Would rather go dancing.'

Colleen ached for the pretty girl. She'd been with them for four months and, like Jake, she'd be going home soon. The staff on the unit had done a charity bungee jump to raise money so that Kiera would be able to take her computer home with her. The rehabilitation unit— the only one of its kind in the south of Ireland—was funded entirely by charitable donations and, although people were generous, there was always a need for more money to buy specialised equipment such as Jake's motorised wheelchair and Kiera's computer. At the moment the coffers for equipment was running very low.

'And the blog? How's that doing?' Colleen had asked.

'A hundred hits a day,' Kiera had typed. When Kiera

had mastered the computer she'd complained of being bored. There was only so much she could do to keep herself occupied. Colleen had suggested she start a blog for other spinal-injury patients. Kiera had eagerly taken to the idea and it had been an immediate success.

Thirty minutes later, having changed in to her civvies, Colleen was ready to leave. In reception, Frobisher was still pacing up and down and looking at his watch with barely concealed impatience. She'd forgotten that he was waiting to see her.

'I'm Colleen McCulloch,' Colleen said. 'You wished to see me?'

Frobisher stopped his pacing and glanced at his watch pointedly.

'Sorry for keeping you waiting,' she said, slipping on her jacket.

He held out his hand. His grasp was firm. 'Daniel Frobisher. Look, is there somewhere we can talk?'

He was so tall she had to tip her head back just to meet his eyes.

'I'm afraid you've wasted your time coming here. The answer is still no. I already told your Mr Haversham I can't take on the care of your son. I'm sorry, but as you can see, I already have a job. I did give him a couple of other names to try.'

'I've taken time I could ill afford to come here, so I think you could at least hear me out.' There was no mistaking the impatience in his voice and Colleen felt herself prickle.

Before she knew what was happening, Frobisher grabbed her by the elbow and was steering her out of the ward. 'I can't stay in this place,' he said tersely. 'I've had enough of hospitals to last me a lifetime. Is there somewhere else we could go to talk?'

'As I said, there's nothing to talk about.' Colleen tried to pull her arm out of his grasp, but his grip was too strong. Was he planning to abduct her? From the grim look on his face she wouldn't put it past him.

She told herself not to be ridiculous. He was hardly going to bundle her into a car in full view of half of Dublin.

But that was exactly what he did. His car, all sleek black and chrome with darkened windows, was waiting right outside the front door of the hospital, where nobody, absolutely nobody, not even Mr Sylvester, the head of the unit, was allowed to park. She was in the back of the car alongside Frobisher so fast she hadn't even had a second to call for help.

He was really beginning to annoy her, sick son or no sick son. She tried the handle of the door as the chauffeur-driven car moved off.

'Would you please stop this car and let me out. This minute!' Colleen tried to keep her voice steady. 'Driver! Stop the car. Immediately.' She scrabbled in her bag looking for a weapon, but all she could find in the jumble of used tissues and coins was a notebook, a pen, her purse and a bottle of perfume. She pulled it out and brandished the bottle at him. 'If you don't, I'll spray you.'

Instead of letting her out, Frobisher pressed a button and a glass screen swished up between them and the driver. 'You're going to disarm me with perfume? Then what? Do the same to my driver?' Amusement flickered in his green eyes and softened the severity of his angular face. 'All I need is thirty minutes of your time.' His eyes grew solemn. 'I promise I'll bring you back as soon as we've talked. All I want is for you to hear me out before you make up your mind.'

Something in the way he said the words, the unexpected timbre of sadness in the tone, made her pause and look more closely at him.

Despite his astonishing good looks there were lines around his eyes and a tightness to his mouth as if he were unused to smiling. Instinctively she knew that this man was in pain. A whole lot of pain. Not that it excused his high-handed behaviour, but she could at least spare him a few minutes.

'Very well,' Colleen conceded reluctantly. 'I'll listen to what you have to say—not that I think it will make much difference, mind. But I'm not going to do it here. I'm starving. I missed my tea break and if I don't have something to eat soon I'll probably pass out on the floor of this car. There's a café I go to all the time just around the corner. Tell your driver to stop there.'

'You promise you won't try to run away?'

Colleen smiled at the image of her running down the streets of Dublin with this man hot on her heels. If there was a more unlikely scenario, she couldn't think of one. 'I promise. I'll give you as long as it takes for me to eat. But that's it.' She held out her hand. 'Do we have a deal?'

Cool fingers pressed hers. Yikes! Did the man have a buzzer in his hand? Something had to have caused the electric shock that ran up her arm. Quickly she pulled her hand away.

When he saw the café a look of astonishment crossed his face. Admittedly, the café wasn't much from the outside, but inside it was warm and cosy and sold the best Irish breakfasts this side of Dublin. Colleen often stopped there on her way to or from home or work—not least because her best friend, Trish, owned the place.

'Are you sure you want to eat here?' Daniel said doubtfully. 'I could suggest somewhere else.'

There was no way she was going to drive any further with this man.

'It's either here or nowhere,' Colleen said firmly. 'It's only a five-minute walk home for me from here. And I need my bed.'

As soon as the words were out of her mouth she regretted them. She didn't want to give him any clues to where she lived. She had the uneasy feeling that he would have no compunction about staking out her flat once she had made him realise that she was serious about not taking the job.

'Okay, you're the boss.' Then he smiled. It was only the briefest smile, vanishing almost before Colleen was sure she had seen it, but in that millisecond his face was transformed, making him look younger and, if possible, even more devastatingly good looking.

The windows of the café were steamed up from the combined breaths of customers filling up on Trish's renowned breakfasts before setting off for work or college. Trish scurried over to them as soon as they were seated in Colleen's favourite place by the window. Behind Frobisher's back, Trish wriggled her eyebrows and pretended to fan herself with her hand.

'I'll have my usual, please, Trish,' Colleen said, pretending not to notice.

'And you, sir?' Trish was practically drooling.

'Coffee. Black. No sugar.'

With a wink at Colleen, Trish sashayed away. Frobisher didn't even look at Colleen's friend. He had to be really worried about his son not to. Trish was gorgeous and most men fell instantly in love with her as soon as they set eyes on her. She was always fending off wannabe suitors.

'Okay. You asked me to listen to you so I'm all ears—

though to be honest, I can't think there's anything you can say to me to convince me.' She softened her tone. 'As I told Mr Haversham—and you—I already have a job here. A job I just happen to love and have no intention of leaving. Besides he told me your home is in London. I'm afraid that in itself makes it impossible. Even if I weren't working already, I couldn't leave Ireland. So you see, you've wasted your time coming out here, Mr Frobisher.'

'Call me Daniel.'

'Daniel, then. Have you tried an agency? From what Mr Haversham told me, your son needs round-the-clock care. There are one or two excellent units in London that I could recommend.'

Trish came back with two coffees and a plate of egg, sausages, bacon and toast. Daniel's expression changed to one of mild incredulity. Had the man never seen a woman eat before? As Colleen added enough ketchup to her satisfaction and speared a slice of sausage on her fork, Daniel fished a photograph out of his top pocket and handed it to Colleen. She set aside her knife and fork and studied the picture. It was of a beautiful woman with blonde hair and shining eyes. It had been taken on a beach with the sun setting in the background. The woman had her arm around a boy who was smiling self-consciously into the camera. Judging by the brilliant green eyes, which were exact replicas of the ones staring intently at her, there was no doubt whose child he was.

'That was taken just over two years ago,' Daniel said softly, 'when my son, Harry, was ten.'

Haversham had told her Harry Frobisher was twelve. Didn't Daniel have a more recent photograph of his son, or was this simply his favourite one?

'That's your wife with Harry?'

'My ex-wife. We were divorced. Eleanor was killed outright in the accident that injured my son.'

'I'm so sorry.' Colleen had to stop herself from reaching out and laying a comforting hand on his. Instinctively she knew the gesture would not be welcome.

Daniel's expression was unreadable. 'She had just collected Harry from his boarding school when it happened. They were on their way to the airport...' He hesitated as if his thoughts were turning inwards, reliving the horror.

'And your son was badly hurt?' she prompted gently.

Pain flashed across Daniel's face. 'Harry's injuries were severe. He was in a coma for almost a week. For a time I thought he wasn't going to make it.' Daniel's voice had become clipped, almost as if he were talking about something that had happened to someone else.

'Harry regained consciousness a month ago. He can't talk and his movement is limited.' Daniel's mouth twisted. 'For God's sake, he can't even feed himself. My child is a prisoner in his own body.'

'It's early days yet,' Colleen said softly. 'He could improve a great deal in the next six months—with the right kind of care.'

Daniel took the photograph from her hands and placed it carefully back in his pocket.

'So they tell me. But I'm not convinced he wouldn't do better at home, getting individual attention from someone with your reputation. I don't just want good care for my son; I want him to have the best. From everything I've learned about you, I believe you are the person he needs. I understand you were a physiotherapist before you became a nurse. I also understand that you specialise in looking after young patients and have had personal experience of this kind of injury.'

Colleen paused, the forkful of egg and toast halfway to her mouth. 'How do you know that?'

'Let's just say that I did my research.' He studied her calmly. 'I would never offer anyone a job without checking them out. You trained at Guy's. I asked Professor Ludwig and without any hesitation he recommended you. I believe if anyone can fix my son, it's you. And I'm prepared to do anything, pay anything, to make that happen.'

'*Fix* your son?' His choice of words chilled her. What—as if he was a broken car or something? Nevertheless, she spoke as gently as possible, knowing from experience that parents sometimes took years to accept their child's prognosis. 'I'm afraid it's not as easy as that. Even if he gets six months of intensive care and rehabilitation, it doesn't mean he'll ever make a full recovery. He may never be the child he once was. In fact—and you should be prepared for this—it's *unlikely* he'll be the child he once was. A brain injury that kept Harry in a coma for a week must have been pretty severe.'

Daniel leaned across the table and fixed his startlingly coloured eyes on Colleen. 'At least say you'll think about it.'

God, she hated it when people put pressure on her. Despite her unease about the way this man chose to go about finding someone to look after his son, she couldn't help but feel sorry for him. No one should have to go through what Daniel was going through. She knew that better than most. Ten years ago, her youngest brother, Cahil had been in the same situation as Harry. That's why she did what she did. But however much compassion she felt for Harry, what Daniel was asking was impossible.

'I'm sorry—the answer is still no.' Colleen pushed the last piece of sausage around her plate and dunked it in tomato sauce. 'Look, I'm sorry about your son, really I am. But I've got a job and I can't just up and leave. And I've got a life here in Dublin—a fiancé, my family…'

'Three brothers—' Daniel's green eyes bored into hers '—two of whom still live at home. Your youngest brother, Cahil, suffered a head injury ten years ago. I believe he's now his school's football-team star striker.'

For the first time in as long as she could remember, Colleen was speechless.

'You're engaged to your childhood sweetheart, Ciaran, but don't live together,' Daniel continued. 'You've started to build your own house and when you have enough money to finish it then you'll get married. Some may think that's old fashioned…' he paused '…unusual, even.'

Anger knotted in her stomach. To think she'd felt sorry for him! Research into her suitability as a nurse for his son was one thing—even if she hadn't applied for the job—but digging into her personal life? That was too much.

'How dare you snoop into my life…?'

'I prefer to call it research and I dare because I want to do what is best for my son.'

'No doubt you do—but it still doesn't give you the right to—'

'You could get a six-month sabbatical from your job. What I'm willing to pay you will be more than enough for you to finish building your house, with plenty left over for a wedding. In addition, I'm also prepared to make a substantial contribution to your rehab unit. I looked into their accounts and my donation would enable them to buy some much-needed equipment. I've spoken to your boss and he's agreed to release you for up to six months—by the way, he has nothing but praise for your nursing skills. As far as being separated from your fiancé and your family is concerned, you'll have as much time off as you need once Harry is on the mend and I'll even arrange a private plane to fly you back to Dublin whenever you want.'

Colleen let out a whoosh of air and sat back in her seat. 'You've thought of everything haven't you?'

'I've had to. For Harry's sake, I will do whatever it takes to make him better.' Daniel swallowed and for a second the mask slipped again and she saw such naked pain in his eyes that she sucked in a breath.

'My son needs me,' Daniel continued. 'And I need you. Help me get my son back. Don't think of doing it for me, if that makes it easier. Think of doing it for him.' For a few seconds silence hung between them. 'Please.'

Colleen studied him for a moment. She had the impression that this man wasn't used to pleading. His insistent green eyes and his obvious distress about his son drew her in, making her want to help him, but still she hesitated. He was asking a great deal and she didn't know enough about Harry to know whether she was the right person for the job.

Daniel pulled another photograph from his pocket. 'This was taken three weeks ago.'

Colleen took the second photograph from him. Harry was lying in a hospital bed. Despite the tube running from his nostril he still looked beautiful with his silver-blond hair and smooth pale skin. Her stomach twisted at the blankness in his green eyes.

Her mind spiralled back to those early days when

Cahil had been injured. He, too, had lain in a hospital bed, looking up at them with unseeing eyes. The doctors hadn't held out much hope. But Mammy had refused to give up on her child. She had insisted on taking Cahil home and as a family they had worked around the clock to coax him back to health. It had taken months to get him to feed himself and even longer before he was walking and talking again, but now, as Daniel pointed out, he was recovered enough to play for the school football team.

Daniel must have seen her hesitation. 'At least say you'll meet him,' he pressed. 'Come to London with me. If, after you've met him, you still feel you can't take up my offer, I promise you, there will be no hard feelings. Your unit will get its donation irrespective of what you decide.'

Before she had a chance to answer, Daniel's mobile rang. He looked at it and frowned. 'I'm sorry, but I really have to take this.' He stood up and headed for the door. 'I'll just be a few minutes.'

As soon as he'd stepped outside, Trish scurried over to the table and sat down opposite Colleen.

'Who the hell is that gorgeous hunk of flesh? Why haven't you told me about him? God, Col, I didn't know you had it in you!'

Colleen's head was still full of images of Cahil and Harry. She shook her head to clear it and looked outside to where Daniel was talking on his phone.

'What? Oh, that's Daniel Frobisher. He wants me to go to London to be his son's private nurse.'

Trish looked disappointed. 'I thought he was your new lover.'

Colleen knew she shouldn't really be shocked. Trish

always said the first thing that came into her head. She glared at her best friend.

'Have you forgotten I'm engaged?' she said, indignant.

Trish let out a whoosh of air. 'And have you forgotten about the doubts you've been having? That in itself is a good reason to go to London. It will give you space to make up your mind about how you really feel about Ciaran.'

Perhaps Trish was right. Ever since she and Ciaran had become engaged, Colleen had been feeling unsure. She should be on top of the world, instead of feeling as if she was being dragged towards a deep hole.

'It's only pre-wedding jitters,' Colleen said, more emphatically than she felt. 'I do love Ciaran, of course I do. I feel comfortable with him. Isn't that what marriage is about? Mutual respect, shared interests...?' She glanced towards where Daniel was standing, still talking into the phone. She couldn't imagine anyone feeling comfortable with him. He was too intense, too restless, too... Just too much of everything!

'Heavens to glory, girl!' Trish said. 'Feeling comfortable with someone is not a basis for marriage. If you want comfort, why don't you buy yourself a pair of slippers? Oops, I forgot. You do have slippers. Those crazy things that look like you're wearing two dead lambs on your feet. Where's the excitement with you and Ciaran? The glamour? The passion? The can't-keep-your-hands-off-each-other kind? Where's the drinking champagne at lunch time?'

'I don't like champagne,' Colleen said with another nervous glance outside. If Daniel came back inside, he'd hear everything Trish had to say. Her friend was in full flow and Colleen knew she wouldn't stop until she'd had her say. 'I prefer tea, as you well know.'

'See! That's exactly what I mean. You don't *have* to like champagne to drink it. Most people drink it because they like the bubbles and because it makes them act all silly.'

'I don't like acting silly.'

Trish's expression grew serious. 'No, you don't. You used to, though. Now you never let your hair down. Life is supposed to be fun, Col. Look, I'm not saying Ciaran isn't a nice guy, but nice is the operative word. You need someone to pull you back out of that safe, cosy, insular world you choose to live in these days. How old are you, Col? Twenty-six? And have you travelled, made wild, passionate love on a beach, bought a pair of shoes you couldn't afford because they made you feel a million dollars? No, you wear bunny slippers and dress like a farmer's daughter most of the time and your idea of a big night out is a trip to the local pub to play pool with Ciaran and your brothers. Not exactly the romance of the century, is it?'

Colleen squirmed in her chair. God, Trish made her and Ciaran sound so boring. It was too much, even from Trish!

'But I am a farmer's daughter. Anyway Ciaran likes me the way I am.'

'You're a beautiful woman, Col; anyone would give their eye teeth to look like you—which is stunning, God help the rest of us—whatever you chose to wear. But when was the last time Ciaran looked at you? I mean, *really* looked at you?'

Instead of Ciaran's face, an image of dark green eyes, drilling into hers, flashed into her head. She glanced outside. It was clear Daniel was coming to the end of his call. She had to shut Trish up before he came back inside.

'I wouldn't dream of making love on the beach,' she hissed. 'Sand would get everywhere and someone might see. But of course, if I wanted to, I could do that with Ciaran. We might yet.'

The door swished open and Daniel was walking towards them. Trish stood up and bent over Colleen.

'The question is, *do* you want to?' she whispered.

Colleen was feeling decidedly unsettled when Daniel sat down in the chair Trish had just vacated. Unwelcome though Trish's word were, they only echoed what Colleen had been thinking these last few months. Perhaps Trish was right and Daniel's offer was just what she needed? Time, on her own, to think.

'I'm sorry about that,' he said. 'I didn't expect the call to take so long.' He smiled at her and unaccountably her heart thumped against her ribs. 'Have you had time to come to a decision?'

Damn! Why did the way he looked at her make her feel as if they were the only two people in the room?

Daniel's green eyes brought back the image of Harry lying on the hospital bed. Colleen's heart twisted. She knew she couldn't walk away, not without meeting Harry at the very least. Ciaran always said she was a soft touch.

'I'll come to London and meet your son,' she said, finally. 'I'll make my decision then. However, if, for any reason, I don't think I'm the best person to care for your son, either because he doesn't react well to me, or because I think he'll be better off in a rehab unit, then I won't take the job. Is that understood?'

There was no mistaking the relief on Daniel's face. 'In that case,' he said, signalling for the bill, 'shall we get going?'

CHAPTER TWO

'GET going? What now? Right this minute?'

'No time like the present. I need to know whether you're going to take the job. You're off duty for the weekend, aren't you?'

Was there anything he didn't know about her life?

Daniel was flicking through his wallet, otherwise he would have noticed that Colleen's jaw had dropped. She closed it quickly.

'I can't go *right now.*'

'Why not?'

'Because I need to pack, make a couple of calls, have a sleep.' She couldn't just go to London at the drop of a hat. Trips needed careful planning. 'Besides don't you need to make plane reservations?'

Daniel dropped a twenty-pound note on the table and, without waiting for his change, took Colleen's elbow and steered her towards the door. This elbow-steering thing he had was beginning to get out of hand. She cast a desperate glance at Trish who grinned and held two thumbs up. So no help there then.

'I have a plane. It's waiting for us at the airport. I'll take you home and you can pick up anything you might need. You can sleep on the plane.'

'But..' Her voice come out as a squeak.

Daniel held the door open and ushered her out. He stopped and stared down at her with his mesmerising eyes. 'Look, you agreed to meet Harry. The hospital wants to discharge him on Monday, Tuesday at the latest. If I don't take him home, they'll transfer him to the nearest rehab unit and I'm not having that.' He smiled tightly. 'I promise you, I'll have you back home tomorrow at the latest.'

He opened the car door and once again she was bundled inside. But there was no reason she could think of, apart from the ones she had raised and he'd swept aside, not to go with him. Ciaran was going to Wales with her brothers for the weekend to watch some rugby match. It hadn't even occurred to him to ask her whether she wanted to go, too. Not that she did, but it would have been nice to be asked. Come to think of it, when had she and Ciaran last done something on their own? Something on the spur of the moment, something romantic? Once more, she felt a sinking sensation in the pit of her stomach.

'Okay, I'll come, but I have to go home and collect some stuff first.' At least Trish couldn't accuse her of not being spontaneous this time. Truth was, it felt good. Exciting. She would text Ciaran and let him know she was going to London. Maybe that would rock him out of his complacency.

'Good girl,' Daniel said. 'Where to?'

Good girl! What was she—a puppy?

Colleen gave him the address and, as the car moved away, she sent Ciaran and her mother a quick text telling them she was going to London and would call them later. Colleen usually went home for her days off, even when Ciaran wasn't there, but wasn't Mammy always telling her that she should stay in Dublin and enjoy herself with her friends sometimes? Why was everyone so determined to tell her to enjoy herself? It wasn't as if she went around with a face like a camel's behind all the time. Sheesh!

When the car pulled up outside her flat, Colleen jumped out and ran up the step, telling Daniel she'd be half an hour. To her consternation, when she stopped to open the communal door with her key, she realised that Daniel was standing behind her. The faint scent of expensive aftershave drifted up her nose and she could almost feel the energy vibrating from his body.

For some reason her hand was shaking and she struggled to get the key to work. Daniel leaned over her shoulder. 'Let me,' he said. The touch of his hand on hers sent that electric shock up her arm and she dropped her hand, letting him take charge of the key. Now she was enclosed by the circle of his arms and she had to concentrate hard to stop her breath coming out in gasps. Anyone would think she'd never been close to a man in her life.

'I thought we agreed you would stay in the car,' she said. Annoyingly, despite her efforts, she still sounded breathless.

'Did we?' he said, mildly. 'I don't remember that.'

Daniel followed her up the three flights of stairs to her flat. This time she managed to open the door first time. She turned to him. She didn't want him inside her home. She needed some time to compose herself. 'Thank you. I can cope fine from here.' She thought she managed the note of sarcasm perfectly.

To her dismay he ignored her and followed her inside her studio apartment. Couldn't the man take a hint? But she could hardly order him out of her flat without appearing rude, and she was never rude.

Spying a pair of tights lying discarded on the arm of a chair, she hurried across and scooped them up. Then, through the open door of the bathroom, she noticed her panties and a towel on the floor so she hurried over to scoop them up, too, before shoving the whole lot into the washing machine. Her coffee cup from last night and her supper dishes were still in the sink, but she'd been in a rush to get to work after being held up by a fascinating programme on the television on anteaters.

'Nice place,' he said drily. He picked up a magazine from the floor. *The Bride.* His lips twitched. 'Interesting dress she's wearing.'

Colleen snatched it from his hands and shoved it on top of the pile she'd still to read. It tottered there for a moment before the whole lot slid to the ground, fanning out on a heap on the floor. Knowing her face was probably beetroot, she took a deep breath. She never, ever got flustered. What the heck had got into her?

Daniel grinned at her and for a second she thought her heart had stopped beating.

'I'll be back in a sec,' she said and sought the refuge of her bedroom. She closed the door and leaned against it. *Look*, she told herself, firmly, *he's only a man in a fancy suit, even if he does have a heartbreaking smile.* God, God, God. Where had the last thought come from?

She set about packing her weekend bag, forcing herself to concentrate on remembering everything. Slippers? Check. Clothes, including clean underwear? Check. Toiletries? She'd pick them up from the bathroom on her way out. What else? Did a person need a passport to travel on a private plane?

She poked her head out of the door. Daniel had made

himself comfortable on one of her chairs and was flicking through *The Bride* magazine, an incredulous look on his face.

'Do I need my passport?' she asked.

'Yes. Er...Dublin isn't part of the UK, if you remember?'

Colleen slammed the door shut. Now he'd think her an idiot too! By the time they got to London, he'd probably have decided to employ someone else. But why should she think that? He was interested in her for her professional skills—not interviewing her as a potential wife!

Once her bag was packed, she looked in the mirror to check her hair. She was pale with dark smudges under her eyes, but there was nothing she could do about that. Sleep was what she needed. In her feverish haste to pack her bags so that she could get Daniel out of her flat her hair had come loose from its braid and wisps were falling into her eyes. She grabbed her hair brush and redid the plait, making sure every last one of her unruly locks was contained. Then she added a slick of lipstick and she was ready. Or as ready as she'd ever be. For once she wished she had listened to Trish on one of their many futile shopping expeditions—at least as far as Trish was concerned—and had bought a dress she could have worn. Something that would give her confidence.

Daniel got to his feet when she came back out of her bedroom with the slow indolence of a lion waking up from a sleep.

'I just have to get my wash bag and I'm ready,' she said.

He took her overnight bag from her hand. 'Let's go, then.'

* * *

Daniel slid a look at Colleen as they were driven towards the airport. She wasn't anything like he'd expected.

When she'd turned Haversham down he'd been shocked. No one had ever refused to do something for Daniel before. And the salary—one most people would have found it hard to refuse—hadn't made the slightest difference. Her refusal had made him more determined to secure her services than he'd been before. And he'd been keen then. Especially after the ringing endorsement her old consultant at Guy's had given her. 'She's a tiger,' he'd said, 'and she never gives up. Don't let that innocent face fool you. What Colleen wants, she gets. Nothing and no one stands in the way of Colleen McCulloch when it comes to what is best for her patients. She's not always conventional, but she's always right. That's what makes her special.'

Somehow he'd imagined the redoubtable Nurse McCulloch, whom everyone he'd spoken to had praised to the sky, to look older, to be more severe. Instead she looked like a teenager with her curls escaping from its elastic band and falling in wisps over her face that she constantly and ineffectually tried to tuck back in. He liked the way her mouth turned up at the corners as if in a permanent smile, even the way her eyes flashed when she was annoyed about something. He'd even liked the way her flat looked. Okay, some might say that it looked as if the occupant had been fighting with a pack of wild animals that had found their way into her home, but there was a good feeling about her small flat with its bunches of wild flowers arranged haphazardly in jam jars. It reminded him somehow of his mother's holiday home in Dorset. The memory made his stomach clench. That cottage had been Eleanor and Harry's home until the accident. Now his son was lying in a hospital bed, unaware that *his* mother had died and that all he had left was a father whom he barely knew.

Daniel stole another look at Colleen. He was more determined than ever to have her as Harry's nurse. He hoped to hell she lived up to her reputation.

CHAPTER THREE

So THIS was how the other half lived? Colleen thought, looking around the interior of the plane. If she were honest, a tiny little bit of her was impressed. Only a minuscule bit, mind. The other part of her felt slightly ridiculous having the attentions of a stewardess all to themselves on the tiny, if luxurious, twin-propped plane. And ridiculously under-dressed in her boy jeans and T-shirt, carrying nothing but an imitation designer hand-bag over her shoulder.

Almost as soon as they'd taken off, Daniel had taken out some papers and a laptop. Once she'd had a good look around and got over the excitement of being on a private plane—and she couldn't pretend for the life of her that she wasn't—even if it might make her look like a country bumpkin in Daniel's eyes—she'd fallen asleep.

She'd only woken when Daniel had bent over her and whispered that they were landing and she needed to fas-ten her seat belt. For a moment when she'd opened her eyes, she couldn't remember where she was. She'd been having a lovely dream. A dream where she was behind someone on a horse and they were galloping off some-where. As she stared groggily into Daniel's eyes, she realised with a guilty start that the person on the horse hadn't been Ciaran. It had been someone with green eyes—the man looking down at her, in fact.

She had hidden her embarrassment by escaping to the small onboard toilet and splashing her face with cold water.

When they were escorted through Heathrow airport and towards a sleek, black, stretch limousine. Colleen noticed people nudging each other, puzzlement etched on their faces as they tried to place them. Daniel with his snazzy suit and air of confidence had to be someone famous and as for Colleen, she must be some pop or film star—someone of importance—surely under-dressing to fool the media?

The thought made her smile. She might as well enjoy her moment in the limelight—it was probably the only one she would have until her wedding day.

They sat in silence as they were driven to the hospital. Daniel had his laptop out again and was deeply immersed in whatever he was reading. She'd never met anyone quite so focused on the task in hand before. One minute his attention was completely concentrated on making her do what he wanted, the next minute he was totally engrossed in whatever was on that laptop of his. She simply couldn't make him out. But it was his son that concerned her. How badly had his brain been injured? What was his prognosis? She wouldn't take this job unless she was sure she could help him.

Whizzing along the motorway seeing London city silhouetted in the distance, Colleen felt a thrill of excitement. She'd always planned to come back to London, but somehow the opportunity had never arisen. Ciaran wasn't the adventurous type. He always said that he didn't see the point in travelling to foreign places when you had everything you needed on your own doorstep.

Although she'd never admit it to Trish, sometimes Colleen longed for a bit more excitement. Was she just being foolish for secretly wanting Ciaran to whisk her away to Paris for a weekend? As he'd said, it'd be a waste of money when they needed every penny to get their house finished before the wedding. But a girl could dream, couldn't she?

The car swung sharply to the right, pulling up outside the familiar buildings of Guy's, the hospital where Colleen had trained. She knew from what he'd told her that Harry had been in ITU before being transferred to the high-dependency unit and then to the paediatric ward.

In the ward, posters covered the walls in an attempt to make the unit as cheerful as possible. Every room was a single and a large bright day room filled with toys lead off to the left.

Daniel paused at the very last room and held a finger to his lips. 'We have to go in quietly. Harry gets startled by any loud noise and it unsettles him.'

'Why don't you go in to see Harry, first, while I chat to the nurses?' Colleen suggested. 'Then I'll come in and say hello.'

Daniel nodded briefly and Colleen went to find the nurse in charge of the ward. When she explained who she was and why she was there, she was directed to an office. A woman with short dark hair looked up from her paperwork and held out a hand. 'I'm Sister Lipton.'

Sister Lipton waited until Colleen was sitting down before she continued. 'So you're the person who's to be Harry's private nurse?' she said. 'Mr Frobisher has told us of his plans.'

Colleen didn't bother to correct her. She had yet to decide whether she was going to take Harry on.

'I have to tell you that I think taking Harry home at this point is a mistake,' Sister Lipton continued.

'Can I ask why?'

The nurse frowned. 'Apart from the fact that there are excellent rehab facilities in London, there is the small matter of the fact that Mr Frobisher doesn't seem to know how to interact with his son.'

'Oh?'

'Harry was in ITU for a week with a GCS score of three. During that time Mr Frobisher, perfectly understandably, refused to leave his son's bedside. But instead of talking to Harry, as we suggested, Mr Frobisher mostly spent his time working on his laptop. Furthermore, I gather he caused the nurses some problems with his demands.' She sighed. 'He insisted on bringing in specialists of his own to assess his son. In fact, he had all sorts of demands. Some of them reasonable. Some less so.'

Colleen hid a smile. She had no doubt that Daniel hadn't been the easiest relative to have around. But what Sister Lipton said about Daniel not interacting with Harry was more of a worry. Nursing staff could only do so much; the rest was up to the patient and their loved ones.

'Mr Frobisher tried the same sort of thing when we moved Harry here once the lad was stable,' Sister Lipton continued. 'I'm afraid he and I clashed more than once. In many ways I won't be sorry to see the back of him.'

'But you don't think he should have Harry at home? I can assure you that I've worked with patients like Harry for many years and Mr Frobisher is fully committed to ensuring that Harry receives as good quality care at home as he does here.'

'That may be,' Sister Lipton said. 'But it's Harry's attitude to his father that worries me. When Harry first regained consciousness he was very agitated. As you know, we see that a great deal with patients like Harry, but it didn't take long for us to notice that it was his father's presence that seemed to distress the boy. We asked Mr Frobisher not to spend so much time on the ward. He wasn't happy, as you can imagine, but even he could see he wasn't helping matters. And as we expected, Harry was—and is—much calmer when his father isn't around.'

Colleen decided to let that pass for the moment. She would make up her own mind. As it stood, Daniel was all the family Harry had left. No one should be keeping the pair apart. Besides, she was getting irritated with Sister Lipton's assumption that she knew best. It had been the same when Cahil had been in hospital. No one had wanted Mammy to take him home, but nothing could stop her mother when her mind was made up. It was one of the ways they were exactly alike. And taking Cahil home, surrounding him with the people who loved him most, had been the right thing to do.

'What can you tell me about Harry's treatment and progress to date?' she asked.

Sister Lipton took her through a detailed summary of Harry's medical treatment. 'As far as we can tell, there is no reason why Harry shouldn't make a good recovery over time. There appears to be no lasting damage to his brain. In fact, we're a little surprised that he hasn't progressed quicker. He seems to understand simple instructions, but we'd really be expecting him to be saying more than the odd word by now. He also has some movement, but not as much as we would expect at this stage.'

'We both know that patients even with apparently identical injuries can progress at different rates. No brain injury is exactly the same,' Colleen said. 'I've seen many cases, as I'm sure you have, where recovery is sudden and dramatic. Perhaps this will be the pattern for Harry?'

No doubt Sister Lipton was an excellent nurse but the way she had spoken about Daniel had made Colleen's blood boil. Just like patients, relatives were different when it came to how they dealt with their loved ones' injuries. Perhaps Lipton was the kind of nurse who expected the relatives to treat her with deference. Frankly Colleen preferred the relatives who made it their business to be involved with their child's care. And despite Daniel's high-handedness, she was sure he only wanted the best for his child.

When Colleen had finished speaking to Sister Lipton, she went along to see Harry.

With the blinds drawn, she could barely make out the frail figure lying on the bed in a tangle of sheets. An older woman in a nurse's uniform was checking Harry's blood pressure while Daniel stood looking out of the window.

Careful not to make any sudden noise, Colleen approached the young boy and her heart constricted. Even in sleep, Harry's forehead was creased in a frown. His legs and arms twitched, as if he was being chased by the hounds of hell. Poor mite.

As if sensing her presence, Harry's eyes slowly opened and stared right at her. His eyes were the same startling green as his father's, but where Daniel's were sharp and focused, Harry's were clouded with confusion.

'Hi, Harry,' Colleen said softly, 'My name is Colleen. I'm a nurse and I look after people who have hurt their heads.'

Harry's eyes shifted from Colleen to Daniel and back again.

Keeping her voice as soothing as possible, Colleen continued. 'May I sit down on your bed, Harry? That's great. There's no need to be scared, I'm here because your dad asked me to come and meet you. He loves you very much.'

Mutely, Harry continued to stare at her.

'Harry, I want to hold your hands—is that okay?' She slipped her fingers round his. They felt stiff and cold. 'That's excellent, Harry. Now squeeze as tight as you can, sweetheart. Squeeze as if I've just pinched your MP3 player and all your favourite tunes.'

The minutes passed and still Harry continued to stare at her. Colleen willed him with every fibre of her being to respond. *Please, Harry, come on, you can do it, darling. Squeeze, squeeze.*

She hadn't realised she'd been holding her breath until she felt the slightest of pressure from Harry's fingers. His eyes locked on hers, only for a moment, but long enough for her to see the fear in his eyes. She held the boy's hand until he relaxed and the fear gradually receded. She already knew there was no way she could walk away from this child.

'That's excellent, Harry. Well done. We're going to be great pals, I just know it. In a few days we're going to take you home with us.'

Harry's eyes shifted until he was looking over

Colleen's shoulders. She was aware that Daniel had
come to stand behind her.

'Go!' Harry said clearly.

'What is it, Harry? Do you want me to go?' Colleen
asked.

With an enormous effort Harry raised his hand until
he was pointing at Daniel. It was obvious that he wanted
his father to leave the room.

Colleen turned around. Daniel looked shaken. 'Why
don't you wait for us outside?' she said.

Daniel hesitated. 'Go on,' Colleen said. 'I'll only be
a moment.'

When Daniel left she turned to face Harry again.

'What is it, Harry? Don't you want to go home and
be with your father? I'll be there, too.'

Harry looked at her. A tear slipped from his eye and
Colleen brushed it away.

'Mum,' he said. 'Want Mum.'

'Oh, Harry, I'm so sorry your mum isn't here. But
your dad wants you at home with him. Together we're
going to do everything we can to make you better. You
can speak a little now, so there's no reason your speech
won't come on. And you can move your arm, so with a
bit of work we should be able to get much more movement back. It'll mean hard work, but your dad and I will
be there to help you every step of the way. C'mon, what
do you say? Shall we give it a go?'

Green eyes studied her for a moment. ''kay,' Harry
said finally, before turning away and closing his eyes.

Outside Daniel was pacing up and down, looking as
if he wanted to find something to kick.

'Maybe he should stay here,' he said. 'He clearly
doesn't feel comfortable with me.' It was the first time

Colleen had seen Daniel look anything less than certain and her heart went out to him.

'The brain injury could be causing confusion, or it could be that he simply doesn't recognise you. Patients with head injuries often suffer from memory loss on and off for quite some time. When we get him home and he has his familiar belongings around him, I'm sure he'll settle down.'

A look of relief crossed Daniel's face. 'You said "we". Does that mean you'll take the job?'

'It does. I think I can help.'

Daniel pulled a hand through his hair and studied her. It was a few minutes before he spoke. 'At least I got one thing right. I found you. Thank you for agreeing to stay. Harry needs you.'

And something tells me you do, too, boyo.

'Okay,' she said, 'let's make plans to get your son home.'

CHAPTER FOUR

COLLEEN had flown home later that day on Daniel's plane. Moving to London for what could be months necessitated more than the few belongings she'd packed. And if Harry was to be discharged on Tuesday she needed to be back in London tomorrow evening at the latest. Daniel had offered to send someone to her flat to pack her things for her, but she'd refused. No one was going to trawl through her cupboards except her. After she'd packed and cleared out her fridge, she had phoned Ciaran to let him know what she'd decided. He'd been disappointingly blasé about the fact he wouldn't see her for a few weeks.

She was being daft, of course she was. Ciaran loved her. Just because he didn't create fireworks because he might not see her very often over the next few months was no reason to feel a little…disappointed? Deflated? Unappreciated?

Relieved?

If anything, the last twenty-four hours had deepened the feeling of unease she felt whenever she thought about her impending marriage.

As before, she flew back to London on Daniel's private plane. Her third flight in less than two days. She could get used to this way of travelling. No endless queueing for her bags to be checked, or to go through security or to have her passport examined. Everything happened as if by magic. As soon as she stepped into the arrivals' hall, Daniel's driver was waiting to take her suitcase, his car right outside, so she barely had to walk.

Colleen reached for the car door before the chauffeur had a chance to open it for her. She looked up at him and smiled. 'I'll lose the use of my own arms if I don't use them.'

'Yes, madam.'

'Oh, no. None of that madam stuff. Please call me Colleen.'

'Yes, madam.'

Oh dear.

Suddenly the driver grinned and held out his hand. 'I'm Mike.'

She shook it, feeling relieved. Much more of that madamising malarkey and she would have gone crazy.

They had driven through London before coming to a halt in front of large wrought-iron gates that swung open as if sensing their arrival.

Once again, Colleen got to the door before Mike could do it for her.

'I don't suppose I can carry my own bags?' she said to him.

'No need. They'll be taken up to your room and un-packed for you,' Mike replied, taking her embarrass-ingly bedraggled-looking bags from the boot.

Colleen looked up at the most enormous mansion she'd ever seen. It was like something out of *Country House Rescue*, except she had no doubt that there would be no crumbling plasterwork or peeling paint in Daniel

Frobisher's palace. Hooking her handbag over her shoulder, she skipped up the sweep of steps. As if by magic, the huge front door swung open, revealing a man in his early fifties, wearing the same black suit, white shirt and tie as the uniform of the chauffeur.

'Welcome to Carrington Hall, Miss McCulloch.'

Colleen held her hand out. 'Mr Haversham, I presume?'

The man couldn't have looked more shocked had she attacked him with a deadly weapon. Colleen let her hand drop.

'Mr Haversham is Mr Frobisher's personal assistant. I'm Burton, Mr Frobisher's butler.'

Did people really still have butlers? This felt more and more like she was in a period costume drama.

'Please call me, Colleen. Don't you have a first name, Mr Burton?'

'Just Burton, miss. Please follow me,' the butler said, taking her bags from Mike. 'Mr Frobisher sends his apologies. I am to tell you that he is unable to welcome you personally, but unfortunately he has pressing business to attend to. He says he'll see you at dinner.'

Colleen hid her dismay. Daniel had made all that effort to get her here in the first place, but couldn't spare the time to greet her! If he truly cared about Harry, shouldn't his son and not a business deal be his first priority? The sympathy she'd been feeling towards him faded. If he thought he could hand Harry over to her and leave it at that, he'd made a mistake. She was here to help him care for his son and Daniel's involvement was absolutely critical. She had to make that clear and the sooner the better.

'He had pressing business, did he? Well, I would like

you to get Mr Frobisher on the telephone and let him know that his presence is needed here.'

Burton raised an eyebrow. 'I'm afraid that won't be possible. Mr Frobisher does not care to be interrupted when he's working.' Was she mistaken or did Burton shudder slightly, as if remembering a time when he had made the mistake of interrupting his boss? Well, she wouldn't be so easily intimidated.

'If you could let me have his telephone number, then I'll call him myself.' Colleen scrambled around in her bag for her phone, eventually finding it caught up in some sweet papers. One day she would have to find the time to give her bag a good clear-out. She waved her mobile at Burton. 'Number, please?'

This time, the penguin-suited man did shudder. And folded his arms. And looked at her with unmistakable resolve. 'As I said, Mr Frobisher will see you at dinner. In the meantime, maybe you'd like to see your room?' He looked at her and his lip curled. 'And freshen up. Perhaps change?'

The cheek. There was nothing wrong with her freshly washed jeans and T-shirt. She was here to work—not look like something from a catwalk.

'I'd rather go straight to Harry's room to make sure everything's in order,' Colleen said stiffly. She'd only been here ten minutes and already she was wondering what she'd let herself in for. 'That's why I'm here. I understand from what Mr Frobisher said that his son will be coming home the day after tomorrow. I'm sure there is a fair bit to organise before then.'

Burton jumped back, startled, as she swept past him. The marbled hall with its high-vaulted ceilings and imposing staircase took Colleen's breath away. This was more like the entrance to a private hotel than a house.

But despite the grandeur, it wasn't a place she would call home. It was too dark and gloomy with its wooden panelled walls and deep-green wallpaper.

'But, miss, Mr Frobisher insisted…'

'Mmm…well, see, here's the thing.' Colleen waved a finger in the air. 'I'm here for Harry. Everyone—and I mean everyone—is second in importance to that. So, which way to Harry's room?'

'If you wait here, miss, I'll just get Mr Frobisher for you. He's working from home today,' Burton replied, regaining his composure.

So Daniel wasn't even at work? He was here all the time, yet couldn't be bothered to make the time to greet her. If possible, she felt even more uneasy. None of this matched the little she knew of Daniel. In Dublin and at the hospital, she hadn't doubted for a second that he cared about his son.

She heard Daniel's footsteps on the marbled floor before she saw him. Somehow she'd expected him to be suited and booted again, not wearing faded denim jeans and an open-necked pearl-grey shirt. His dark hair was kind of mussy, as if he'd been pulling his hands through it, and he had the beginnings of a five-o'clock shadow. It made him look more approachable and really quite sexy in an uptight British way.

'Colleen, welcome. Did you have a good flight?' he asked, with only the briefest of smiles.

'Everything about my trip was great, thanks,' Colleen replied, coolly.

'I gather you wish to speak to me. What is so important that it can't wait?'

'I'd like to see Harry's room, but Mr Burton appears reluctant to show it to me. He seems to want to pack me off to my room so I can change. I tried to tell him that I don't need to rest or change or freshen up, or whatever it is that he seems to think I need to do, but he's not having it. I'm not in the least bit tired, I'm almost as clean as I was when I showered this morning and I want to see Harry's room. Is that a problem?'

A smile, more genuine this time, crossed Daniel's face.

'Of course not. Burton was just following instructions. Guests normally like to settle in to their rooms when they arrive.'

'But I'm not a guest, sure I'm not.'

Something glinted in Daniel's eyes. If she didn't know better, she would have sworn it was laughter. He regarded her calmly without saying anything. She already that knew that he wasn't exactly a chatterbox. But if he thought his silence would make her back down meekly, he had another think coming.

'Here's the thing,' she continued doggedly, trying to ignore the way her heart was racing, 'I'm here to do the best job I can for Harry, but in order to do that—what I say goes. Do we understand each other?' Colleen held her breath as she waited for Daniel to reply. Despite the instant connection she'd felt with Harry, she couldn't work here unless she had free rein to do what she thought was best for him. She needed to make that absolutely clear from the start. Daniel studied her through narrowed eyes.

'Perfectly. But let me make something clear, too. If, at any time, I feel you are not up to the job, I will find someone else.'

He was pinning her with that look again. Her heart was galloping like one of the horses in the field back home. Jeepers, life in this household wasn't going to be easy.

'Have you forgotten that you were the one who hounded me to take the job and not the other way round? But that's fine by me, just as long as whatever happens, you don't renege on your donation to the rehab unit.'

'I never go back on my promises, Colleen.' The words were quietly spoken, but held a thread of steel. 'And something tells me you don't either.'

Colleen just couldn't make Daniel out. For two pins she'd insist on being taken back to Ireland. If it weren't for the fact that Daniel was right—she never backed out of a promise. She'd told Harry she'd be here when he came home and she'd keep that promise.

'Despite the way you went about securing my services, I've agreed to care for your son and I would never, ever let my—er—relationship...' *damn, that was the wrong word, but it was too late now to find a better one* '...with a parent affect the way I treat a patient.' And that was true. Even if she'd never felt like kicking someone before.

His smile was catlike. 'At least we understand each other.'

Colleen let her breath out slowly, willing her heart rate to return to normal. 'Okay, now that that's out of the way, shall we get on?'

Daniel looked at his watch. 'It's okay, Burton, I can manage from here.' He turned his gaze back to Colleen. She'd forgotten just how green those penetrating eyes of his were—even when he was frowning. 'I can give you ten minutes. Follow me. Harry's bedroom is on the second floor.'

Colleen remained silent for the rest of the way up the curving stairs and along the carpeted hallway lined with old-fashioned portraits of stuffy men in uniforms and aristocratic women in evening dresses. Daniel threw open the very last room at the end of the long corridor.

'This is Harry's room,' he said over his shoulder. 'I've installed a hospital bed as you can see. You're in the suite next door.'

Colleen glanced round, taking in the bare walls and almost-empty shelves. An electric wheelchair stood in front of the unlit fireplace. She walked over to the bookshelf and tilted her head to the side, reading the titles along the spines: *Great Expectations*, *The Decline and Fall of the Roman Empire*, a couple of other tomes and a raft of other titles she didn't recognise. Either Harry had unusual tastes for a twelve year old or these books didn't belong to him.

She could sense Daniel's impatience as he waited until she'd finished.

'Would you like to see your room now?' he asked.

'There's plenty of time for that later,' Colleen replied.

He shrugged. 'All right. You'll find some uniforms laid out for you.' He gave her an appraising look. 'I'm pretty sure they'll fit perfectly.'

'I'm pretty sure they will, too, but I won't be wearing a uniform.' She pulled the heavy curtains back from the window and gazed down below. It was hard to believe they were in the centre of London—with the greenery in the garden below the concrete buildings of the city seemed miles away. She turned back to face him. 'It's important that Harry feels at home. Me wearing a uniform is not going to give him that impression. He's already spent almost two months in hospital and I doubt he wants to be reminded of his experience there.'

Daniel tipped his head. 'I see your point. It didn't occur to me.' He pulled his hand through his hair—she'd been right in her guess about where the mussy hair came from . 'Clearly, I'm making a pig's ear of this.'

His words, along with his baffled expression, disarmed her. He was after all, a father who wanted the best for his child. But she didn't want to feel sorry for him—she already sensed that there was going to be more than one battle of wills between them. In many ways it was easier to deal with the arrogant, self-assured Daniel of earlier.

'Don't be too hard on yourself,' she said gently, 'you've never been in this situation before.' She took a last look round the room. 'Okay, that's fine—I've seen enough. Could I see the rest of the house, please?'

She followed Daniel back down the stairs and across the vast hallway. He swung open the first door on the right, leading Colleen into a large lounge. Heavily polished rosewood tables complimented several worn chocolate-brown leather couches, which framed an enormous, slightly threadbare Oriental carpet in front of a head-height marble fireplace. Surely with all his wealth Daniel could get a new carpet and some modern furniture? The rug on the floor had clearly seen better days. She pointed to the fireplace. 'Grief, Santa wouldn't have any problem coming down your chimney, would he?'

Daniel didn't answer, but she thought she saw that glint in his eyes again. There was a definite twitch of his lips.

Bay windows streamed in light with a broad view of the lush green garden bursting with flowers and shrubbery that she'd noticed from upstairs.

'As I said in the contract I faxed over to you, there is a heated swimming pool in the basement as well as a gym that you are welcome to use. You may have your meals in your room, or with Harry, or in the dining room. I'll leave that up to you. I've engaged night nurses to look after Harry from eight in the evening to eight in the morning, and you will be free to do whatever you wish between those hours. You may take every second week-end off and my plane will be at your disposal should you wish to go back to Ireland for the weekend. A car will always be available to you—'

'I am able to read, Daniel,' Colleen said with a smile. 'The contract was very detailed.' She paused. 'How easy is it to get down to the pool?'

'It's down a flight of steps and along a corridor.'

'Any chance of getting a lift installed?' she asked. 'Then we could take Harry down to the pool for his physio. A lot of patients find the water makes it easier for them to move their arms and legs.'

'I'll get Haversham on to it straight away. Anything else?'

'What's through the double doors there?' Colleen pointed to the middle of the room.

'The dining room. Look, if you want a tour of the house I'll ask Burton to show you around. I should get back to work. I'm expecting a conference call in...' he glanced at his watch '...five minutes. We can talk later. Over dinner, if you care to join me.'

'Can I see the dining room?'

With a barely concealed sigh of irritation, Daniel waved his hand. 'Help yourself.'

Colleen pushed open the doors and grinned. This room was perfect. 'Daniel, would you come in here, please?'

'What is it?'

'I think this should be Harry's new room.'

'I've just shown you his bedroom—it's what he's fa-miliar with.'

Colleen shook her head. 'It's too far away from the rest of the household. And it will be difficult getting him up and down the stairs.' She pushed open the French doors leading out on to a patio. 'This room will make a perfect bedroom for him.' She swung round. 'If you could arrange to have the furniture cleared out of here straight away so we can get Harry settled in.'

'No.'

'No? What do you mean "no"?'

'Harry is sensitive to noise. There is no way he'd get the peace and quiet he needs down here.'

The silence stretched between them. Clearly when he said he'd give her free rein in the care of Harry, he meant it still had to be on his terms. It was time to change tack. 'I'd kill for some tea—any chance of a cuppa?'

'Sure. I'll get Burton to bring a tray to your room.'

'Can't we have it down here? It's obvious to me that we need to discuss Harry's care in more detail.'

Daniel frowned and looked at his watch—again. 'I really have to take that call. We can discuss whatever it is you wish to this evening.'

'I'm sorry, but that won't work. Harry is coming home the day after tomorrow and we've got to get everything ready for him.' She forced herself to keep her tone as neutral as possible, although frustration and annoyance was beginning to bubble again.

Daniel's expression hardened. 'Everything *is* ready for my son.' His tone was clipped. 'I've made sure of that. All you've got to do is do your job. That's what I'm paying you for.'

This wasn't going to be as easy as she thought. He needed to be reminded that she was a professional and was not prepared to be bossed around.

'Haven't we just had this conversation, Daniel? You

have to trust that I know what I'm doing.' She kept her voice even. 'I wouldn't suggest changes if I didn't think they were important.'

'Forgive me,' Daniel replied with a disarming smile. 'It's just that I'm not used to relinquishing control. And, if I'm honest, I'm just so damned nervous about Harry coming home.'

Colleen found herself smiling back. Of course he was bound to be anxious. No wonder he was being prickly. Anyone would in his situation.

Colleen pulled out one of the high-backed dining chairs and sat down at the mahogany table. Taking her notebook out her bag, she thumbed through it. 'Have you told him what's happening on Tuesday? That that's the day he's coming home?'

Daniel leaned his arms on the back of a chair. 'I did. I don't know how much of it he took in. Sometimes he won't talk at all, so we've worked out a system. One blink means no, two means yes. When I told him I was taking him away from the hospital and you were coming to look after him, he blinked once.' Daniel ran his hand through his hair. 'I have no idea whether that means he doesn't understand or whether that means he doesn't want to come home.'

'It's important not to push him too much right now, but I think if he didn't want to come home, he'd have made that clear.'

Pain flashed in Daniel's eyes. She knew he was re-membering yesterday, when Harry had demanded he leave.

Colleen leaned forwards in her chair. 'With regards to Harry's room, please hear me out before you dismiss my suggestions.' She held up her hand as Daniel looked as if he were about to speak. 'I know you say Harry is frightened of noise, but it's more important that he doesn't feel separated from the rest of the household. If we move his room into the dining room, he'll soon get used to the hubbub; in fact, he will probably find it reassuring. When the weather's good we can open the double doors or take him out to the garden. It will be much easier than installing a lift to take him from the first floor to the basement.'

She waited for him to challenge her again, but to her surprise, he nodded. 'Okay, I can see it's worth a try. If the noise does upset him, we'll move him back to his old room.'

Daniel's unexpected capitulation surprised, but pleased her. She really didn't want to spar with him over every aspect of Harry's care.

'Point two…' she counted on her fingers. 'No hospital bed. Bring Harry's old bed in here or buy him a new one. Three—where are his belongings? You know, such as his computer, MP3 player—the normal things lads his age have. I didn't notice any in his room upstairs.'

Daniel shook his head as if he didn't understand the question. 'Apart from his iPod, which I have, the rest of his stuff is probably still at the house he shared with his mother in Dorset. But Harry isn't able to move, never mind use his computer.'

'Not now, no. But he needs to be surrounded by familiar things, his own things.'

'Fine. I'll arrange that.' He stood up. 'I take it that's all. I've really got to go back into work.'

'Afraid not. Not by a long chalk, so forget about work for a while.' Colleen tapped her pen down her notes. 'What sport does Harry like?'

'Oh, for God's sake!' Daniel swung towards her, hands bent down on the table. 'What kind of question is that? My son...' His voiced cracked. He raked a hand through his hair and turned away from her. Colleen heard his intake of breath as he struggled to regain his composure. 'We don't know if he'll ever walk again, never mind play sport—and I don't want him reminded of that fact.'

'You don't know yet what Harry will be capable of,' Colleen replied softly. 'But you've got to have hope—and you've got to give him hope. Give him goals to aspire to.'

Daniel thrust his hands in his pockets and walked towards the French windows. She waited patiently for him to reply.

Finally he cleared his throat. 'Cricket. Cricket and rugby.'

'Does he follow any special team? Any heroes he admires?'

Still with his back to her, he shook his head. 'I don't know. My wife Eleanor would know—would have known. I took Harry to a cricket match at Lord's once but, well...let's just say it wasn't a great success.'

Colleen stared at Daniel, puzzled. He didn't seem to know very much about his son.

'Does Harry know his mum is dead?' Colleen asked quietly.

This time Daniel did turn round, his startlingly handsome face expressionless. 'He hasn't asked where she is. I don't even know if he's aware of who he is or what's happened to him. I talked it over with the staff and I decided I couldn't tell him. Not yet. Not until he's stronger.'

'That's okay. However, we should be prepared for him to ask at any time. With brain injuries, the loss of memory and confusion can last for weeks, maybe months.

But it can also come back quite suddenly.' Colleen kept her tone matter of fact. 'If you could arrange to get as many of Harry's personal belongings back here, that would be a start. You said that he was attending board-ing school, and it's the school holidays, so maybe you could encourage his friends to visit.'

Daniel puffed out his cheeks, looking relieved that he had something practical to arrange. She had no doubt that he'd be clinically efficient in getting all her rec-ommendations carried out to the letter—now that he'd agreed with them. The next part would be trickier.

Colleen remained seated, signalling that she wasn't quite finished yet. She tilted her chin up and kept her gaze steady as she looked at him. 'I understand you've secured the services of a speech therapist as I requested.'

'Yes. She's ready to come whenever you say the word.'

'And a night nurse to keep an eye on Harry during the night. I am happy to be woken if she needs me, of course.'

Daniel nodded. 'A couple of the nurses from the ward Harry's been on have agreed to do a rotation of shifts on their days off. They'll also cover the weekends when you're back in Dublin.'

'Good. The fewer new faces, the better.' She sat up straighter. 'There's one more member of Harry's team whose role we haven't mentioned yet. In fact, the most important one.'

Daniel frowned. 'I haven't authorised any one else on the payroll, but of course if you can think of anyone we should get to help, that's not a problem.'

'I meant you.'

'Me?' He looked startled 'I don't know the first thing about looking after a child with head injuries—that's why I employed you. I've also got my work. There's no way I can...' He stopped and looked down at her. 'What would you want me to do?'

Colleen sighed. 'Daniel, it's going to be tough, I promise you that. Harry has a long road ahead of him and he'll need you every step of the way. I don't care about your work—that's up to you. But I can tell you that unless you're with Harry, reading to him, playing his favourite music, reminding him of the good times you shared, we may never break through to him.' Colleen held his gaze. 'Harry needs someone to fight for him. He needs *you* to fight for him. Make him believe that he is the centre of your universe—that he matters to you.' She looked at him. 'You asked me to save your son and I'll do everything in my power to help him. But, Daniel, make no mistake—it's you he really needs right now.'

Daniel walked over to the window and stood there without saying anything.

As the silence stretched between them, anxiety coiled in the pit of Colleen's stomach. Did Daniel even understand what she was getting at?

'Needs me?' When he finally spoke, his voice was harsh. 'I wish it were that easy.'

'You love him.' She spoke softly. 'But you need to show him. Trust me, everything else will follow from that.'

He turned around. With the sun at his back, she couldn't read the expression in his eyes.

'Trust you?' he repeated with a short laugh. 'Well, Colleen McCulloch, it seems I have no option but to do just that.'

And before she could think of a response, he walked out of the room.

CHAPTER FIVE

Before Daniel left to make his conference call, he passed Colleen back over to Burton to show her to her room on the first floor. Its size—four times that of her room at home—made her gasp. In the centre was a canopied four-poster, a working fire to her left and a sofa with two chairs. Through a door on her right was an *en suite* bathroom with claw-footed bath that was big enough for two. It felt as if she had stepped back in time to the 1920s.

'Please make yourself at home, miss,' Burton said. 'There is a bell pull by the side of the bed; if you need anything, please ring. Do you have any preferences for dinner?'

'I eat just about anything.' Colleen said. She patted her hips. 'As you can probably tell.' Now why did she say that? It was just that Burton and the whole set up in this house made her nervous.

'Very well, Miss. Afternoon tea is at four in the small sitting room. Dinner is at seven.'

'Thank you, Mr...er...Burton, but I think I'll skip afternoon teas. The hips, you see.' But as the door clicked closed behind Burton, she realised she was speaking to an empty room.

She walked over to the large sash windows and gazed

out at the formal gardens below. In the centre was a statue of a Greek figure holding something in his hand. Could it possibly be Cupid? The thought made her smile. It was unlikely. A statue like that spoke of a whimsy this house didn't have.

She left her bag on the floor and made her way back downstairs. It was deserted. She went in search of Burton, opening door after door to find room after room, beautifully decorated but, like the rest of the house, totally devoid of life. Grand it might be, if slightly out of date, but this house wasn't loved. It was a mausoleum— not a home. So it was up to her to make it welcoming for Harry.

Colleen arched her back and stretched out her aching muscles. The past few hours had been busy. Burton had helped as had Mike, who, finally, had given up with the madam stuff and was now calling her Colleen. Although Burton had tried to persuade her to leave organising the room to him and Mike, Colleen had insisted on staying to make sure every single instruction was carried out to the letter. Even if it meant helping to heave round the furniture so that it was placed to her exact satisfaction.

She stood back and surveyed the once-elegant dining room with a critical eye, finally nodding with approval. Harry's bed had been retrieved from wherever it had been removed to and had been positioned against the back wall in the centre of the room facing the French doors. The heavy brocade curtains had been replaced by neutral curtains that let in more light, making the room less oppressive. Colleen had left the childish posters and books upstairs exactly where they belonged. She'd been out to the garden and brought back masses of fragrant roses to arrange in vases later. Now all she needed was

Harry's things—his current favourite books, posters and games, for a start. They would be at the house in Dorset, no doubt. In that case, Daniel would need to fetch them. She would raise the subject over dinner. Mike had told her that Daniel had gone to visit Harry at hospital. She could have gone, too, of course, but Daniel hadn't even let her know he was going. Any softening she had felt towards him had disappeared again.

After thanking Burton and Mike for their help, Colleen ran up to her room. Someone—it had to be Burton—had somehow found the time to unpack her bags for her, and now her meagre possessions were hanging in the wardrobe, looking a bit lost and forlorn.

The thought of the austere and formidable-looking Burton putting away her underwear made her cringe.

Although it was July and the days were warm, her room had been chilly earlier and someone had thought-fully lit a fire. She walked over and warmed her hands by the flickering flames.

As the firelight bounced off the small diamond in her engagement ring, she wondered if she should give Ciaran a call, but then, almost instantly, decided against it. He'd be totally caught up with the rugby match; besides she didn't really feel like talking to him.

The realisation sent a shiver down her spine. At one time she would have been straight on the phone to him. They would have laughed over Burton's stuffiness and she would have shared the details of her trip and this incredible house. But the truth was, until now, she'd hardly thought about Ciaran. She wrapped her arms around herself, trying to force warmth into her bones. Perhaps it was because events of the last couple of days—her tussles with Daniel and her anxiety to ensure that everything was perfect for when Harry came home—were preoccupying her? But the feeling of unease wouldn't go away. Was Trish right? Was it possible that by marrying Ciaran she was about to make the biggest mistake of her life?

No. She loved Ciaran. Of course she did. It was just pre-wedding jitters. That was all.

At seven she headed back downstairs to be met by Burton.

'Good evening, miss,' Burton said. 'As the main dining room is now out of commission, I have arranged for dinner to be served in one of the other rooms. Mr Frobisher is waiting for you in the library. If you would follow me?'

As if she couldn't find the way herself! However, after being led up one flight of stairs and down another past several rooms before coming to the library, Colleen had to admit that she would have never found the room herself. In fact, a map of the house wouldn't be a bad idea.

Daniel was sitting in a leather chair that faced out over the garden. The room, furnished simply with a couple of leather chairs, a writing desk and floor-to-ceiling shelves of books, was freezing. Daniel clearly didn't feel the cold.

He jumped to his feet when Burton announced her as if she were a guest at a posh wedding.

'Good evening, Colleen. Have you settled in? Please let me know if there is anything we can do to make your room more comfortable.' Now *he* sounded like Burton.

'I've stayed in hotels that are significantly less comfortable than my room,' Colleen said with a smile. Then she decided to get straight to the point. 'What I would like to know is why you didn't tell me you were going to the hospital to visit Harry? Didn't it cross your mind that it might be appropriate for me to come, too?'

'I didn't tell you I was going because I wanted to remind him that you were here first—in case he'd forgotten.'

'It would have been better for him to see me again. The more familiar he is with me before he comes home, the better.'

Daniel's lips formed a narrow line. 'I think you should let me decide what is best for my son at this point.'

'Although you have employed me as the expert?' Colleen didn't even attempt to keep the exasperation from her voice. 'Didn't we just agree that this morning?' She bit her lip, annoyed with herself. She had to keep reminding herself that underneath the cool exterior and piles of money and trappings was a man who was trying to do the best for his son and was scared to death of doing the wrong thing. She had to tread as gently with the father as she would with Harry if she was to have any hope of doing a good job.

However, there was something she needed Daniel to do before Harry came home.

'We've moved Harry's room into the dining room as we discussed,' she said.

'So Burton tells me.'

'But the room is bare. Would it be possible to go to the home he shared with his mother and bring back his stuff from there? We might be able to recreate a room for him here that feels familiar. What was his room in Dorset like?'

'I'm afraid I have no idea. I've only been there once in the last couple of years.'

Colleen tried to hide her astonishment, but if Daniel noticed he didn't so much as betray it by a flicker of his eyelids. 'However,' he continued, 'there is nothing to stop me having Mike fetch Harry's belongings. He could do it tomorrow.'

'I would like to go myself,' Colleen said. 'It will give me a feel of what Harry was like before his accident. In fact, I think we should both go.'

'I can't. I'm afraid I have meetings tomorrow.' This time there was a flicker of something in his eyes, although what it was, Colleen couldn't say. Irritation? Embarrassment? Guilt? For sure, he should be embarrassed. So far, from what she could gather, Daniel knew very little about his son and, despite everything he'd said, didn't seem particularly keen to get involved with him. But to be fair, there could be all sorts of reasons for him not visiting the home where his son lived. Perhaps relations between him and his ex-wife had been strained. He wouldn't be the first parent who had to collect his child for visitation rights from neutral territory. On the other hand, perhaps he had still been in love with his wife. Maybe the thought of seeing her had been too difficult. Nonetheless, whatever the reason for his reluctance, it was important that Daniel come with her.

'I really think we should both go,' she insisted.

Daniel stood up and took a couple of steps towards her. He looked as if he'd just stood on some chewing gum and it had stuck to his foot and he was looking for the perpetrator and, boy, when he found him, he was going to sort him out.

'Good God, Colleen. Are you going to challenge me at every turn? I am Harry's father,' Daniel said. 'In the end the ultimate responsibility for his well-being rests with me.'

Colleen had to dig her nails into her palms to stop herself from retorting that so far he didn't seem to have a clue what was best for his son. And she was damned if she was going to let him intimidate her. She jumped to her feet, too, but immediately regretted it when Daniel took a step towards her. She had forgotten how tall he was, how unnerving his eyes were. Despite every instinct telling her to back down, she held her ground. 'And I thought I made it clear that as long as I am to be Harry's nurse, I will decide what is in your child's best interests as far as his rehab is concerned.'

For a long moment the air between them seemed to shiver. Colleen held her breath.

Suddenly and quite unexpectedly Daniel grinned and Colleen's heart did something very peculiar inside her chest. He really was the most astonishingly good-looking man. If only he would smile more often, perhaps people would be more likely to do as he asked.

'I'm sorry. That was unforgivably rude of me. You are absolutely right. I employed you because I believe that you do know what you're doing. I guess I'm not very good at deferring to someone else when it comes to making decisions. But give me time.'

Once again he seemed completely different to the person who'd been glowering at her a few moments earlier. What was it with this man that made her feel constantly wrong-footed? One minute she was ready to hate him, the next, he made her feel all mushy inside. It must be because she felt sorry for him. Well, not sorry exactly. Daniel wasn't the kind of man a person felt sorry for. Empathetic? No. Sympathetic! That was the right word. Any soft feelings she had were because she *sympathised* with him. Now she'd sorted that inside her head, she felt better.

He reached out and before she knew it his hand was at the back of her head. She felt a sharp tug, then her hair was released from its ponytail and falling around her shoulders. 'That's better. Now you don't look quite as fierce.'

He was laughing at her. Colleen felt her cheeks redden, but whether it was from anger or something else, she didn't want to think about. All she knew was that this man made her feel off balance—and she wasn't used to feeling that way. She reached out and grabbed her scrunchie, tied her hair back into its ponytail and regarded him steadily.

'If it's all the same to you, I think I'll have dinner in my room tonight.' She was pleased to hear that her voice sounded normal. 'I'm tired and we have a long day in front of us tomorrow. I'll be ready to set off for Dorset no later than eight tomorrow. Shall I meet you in the hall?'

He was still grinning, but there was something disturbing in his smile... Something that sent a shiver down her spine, because her reaction to his smile wasn't something a woman who was engaged should be feeling. What on earth was the matter with her? She had to be overtired and that was making her over-emotional. Relief made her feel light headed. Really, it was obvious when she thought about it.

'Eight o'clock tomorrow it is,' Daniel said and opened the door for her. He bent his head to hers. 'Are you sure you won't change your mind about dinner?' His breath fanned her neck and little goose bumps popped out all over her body.

'No, thanks,' she said formally, and, resisting the impulse to bolt from the room, she bade him goodnight with what she hoped was a nonchalant smile and walked away.

CHAPTER SIX

UNTIL she saw Daniel pacing the hall at exactly eight the next morning, Colleen hadn't been sure whether he'd keep his word. She had fully expected to find Burton meeting her to tell her that Daniel had been called into work and that Mike would be taking her instead. But as Daniel was wearing jeans and a casual short-sleeved shirt, it seemed he had decided to take the day off work after all.

A team of contractors were busy working in the hall. Daniel hadn't wasted any time getting the lift organised. He was deep in conversation with a man who appeared to be the foreman.

As she waited for him to finish, she hid a yawn behind her hand. Last night, she had tossed and turned, unable to sleep for wondering what she had let herself in for. She kept replaying that moment when he'd let down her hair and her disturbing reaction to him.

When he saw her in the hall, he came towards her. His eyes were shadowed as if he too had spent most of the night awake.

'As I'm going to be unavailable for most of the day, I spent most of the night on conference calls with America. Thank God, they're awake when most of the UK is asleep,' he said as if he'd read her mind. She hoped to hell he couldn't. There were all sorts of way-ward thoughts rattling around in there.

'Wouldn't want you to miss out on a business deal now, would we?' Colleen muttered under her breath, but Daniel had already turned away and was issuing a stream of instructions to Burton who was standing by the door waiting patiently with both their coats in his hand.

'Shall I expect you both for dinner, sir?' Burton asked in his mournful voice that by now Colleen was realising was the way he always spoke. God, she'd love to see him crack a smile. Did no one in this house have anything to be happy about? Then she felt ashamed. Of course they didn't. Not too far from here was Daniel's son, who was severely injured, and as Burton had obviously come with the bricks, he had probably known the late Mrs Frobisher well.

'It's a two-hour journey to Dorset and another two hours back,' Daniel said. 'I don't know how long we'll need to spend at the house, but I hope to be back in time for evening visiting at the hospital. Ask Mike to meet us down at the house with one of the cars. Tell him to bring the Bentley. We'll need the boot space.'

So Daniel had a Bentley? It wasn't the kind of car she associated with him. Surely Daniel was more of a Porsche man?

And it seemed she was almost right. The car waiting outside wasn't a Porsche—it was some other equally sleek sports car, but it was definitely more in keeping with what she knew of Daniel. *Which was exactly what?* she thought. *A big fat zero, more or less. How many cars did he have, anyway?* She decided to ask him as Burton helped her into the passenger seat of the car as if she were completely unable to move her own legs.

'No idea,' Daniel answered her question as they sped

away with a spurt of gravel. 'Six? Seven? I don't know and I don't particularly care. I inherited them from my father. He collected cars. They're mostly kept garaged at the house in Cambridgeshire.'

'How can you not know how many cars you have?' Colleen said. 'And Mike told me you have, what is it, four houses? I would have thought that two max was enough for most people.'

'I imagine you have an opinion on most things,' Daniel said, sounding amused.

Colleen smiled. 'My brothers are always saying that I should give people a chance to speak before I rush in and tell them how I see it.'

Daniel smiled back and the tension in the car eased as he weaved his way through the London traffic, pointing out various landmarks as they went along.

When they reached the motorway, he turned on the radio and fiddled with the buttons until he found a station playing classical music.

'This okay for you?' he asked.

'Actually I prefer country and western myself,' Colleen said. She slid him a glance and smiled again. 'I did admit to having an opinion on most things.'

Daniel caught her look and his lips twitched.

'But I also like rock—you know, the golden oldies— as well as more contemporary artists,' Colleen continued hastily. She preferred it when he didn't look at her like that, as if she were an intriguing creature from another planet.

Daniel found a station to satisfy them both and for the next hour and half they sat in silence, each wrapped in their own thoughts.

* * *

'So you're getting married?' Daniel said suddenly. 'Have you decided on a date?'

'No, not yet. But with the salary I'll be earning, I'm hoping for an autumn wedding.'

'You don't sound very excited.'

Didn't she?

'But I am excited!' Colleen protested, the words not sounding convincing even to her own ears. 'We've been waiting for this day to come around for so long. We've even started building a house.'

'What does he do? Your fiancé.'

Colleen slid a look in his direction. 'I thought you knew everything about me. You had me *investigated*, after all.'

His green eyes glittered back at her and she felt that strange sensation in her stomach again. Maybe she should stop looking into his eyes?

'My research didn't include your fiancé.'

'Ciaran works on the family farm with my brothers.' Colleen decided it was time to change the subject. The discussion was bringing back that sinking feeling in the pit of her stomach. And she wasn't here to talk about herself. She was here to do a job and that meant finding out everything she could about Harry and his life before the accident.

'Were Harry and his mother close?' she asked.

'Of course. Aren't all mothers and sons?'

Colleen bit back the retort that rose to her lips. Not all mothers and sons. Certainly not all fathers and sons. Wasn't this man sitting next to her living proof of that? He seemed completely oblivious to the irony in his last statement.

'I mean, Harry was at boarding school before his accident, right? How did he like it?'

Daniel looked puzzled. 'I'm pretty sure he liked it well enough. I wanted him to have the best education money could buy. It's the same school I went to and my father before me. It never did me any harm. In fact, it toughened me up. Made me self-reliant and confident.'

Colleen choked back the words that came to mind. In her opinion it explained a lot.

'And Eleanor was happy about this?'

'It was her idea. She'd been to boarding school herself and the best local schools were over-subscribed. Of course she missed him, but we both agreed it was for the best.'

Best for whom? Colleen wondered. She couldn't see how it was best for a young child to be sent to live with a bunch of strangers. It wasn't as if Harry even had a brother there to help him through the inevitable homesickness. She remembered the time her youngest brother had gone away with the scouts on a two-day camp. He'd phoned home on the first night and insisted their parents come and fetch him home.

'Eleanor thought he'd have company there,' Daniel continued. 'Harry was shy, or so she said. She thought it would give him confidence to be with others his own age.'

Even worse. Sending a shy, lonely boy away from home—how could anyone think that was the right thing to do? However, she wasn't going to voice her opinion. Not now at any rate. Daniel was hurting enough as it was.

'He came home every weekend. Mostly to his mother and the cottage in Devon. A couple of times to Carrington Hall.' He pulled his hand through his hair in that characteristic way Colleen was beginning to learn meant he was baffled. 'After the second time, he refused to come again. Probably because there was no one of his own age to play with, I guess.'

Colleen's heart went out to Harry. She could see the little boy wandering around that big house looking for company and not finding it. No wonder he stopped wanting to come. Hadn't the same thought crossed his father's mind?

'He was only at boarding school for the last two years. He was at day school until he came back to the UK,' Daniel said.

'Came back to the UK?'

Daniel's fingers tightened on the steering wheel. 'Harry was born in Buenos Aires. He lived there with his mother and stepfather. They only returned to the UK when Harry was ten.'

Colleen waited for him to continue, but it was a few minutes before he did.

'Harry's mother and I divorced before Harry was born. She took him to Buenos Aires with her and the man she married when our divorce came through. Eleanor and David separated when Harry was nine. That was when she decided to bring him back.'

That made it worse. Couldn't Daniel see? Not only was Harry in an unfamiliar place, but he'd also been separated from the man who he'd known as his father for most of his life. Although it explained why Daniel didn't seem to know his son very well, there was something that didn't quite add up.

'But you visited Harry in Buenos Aires?'

Daniel's jaw clenched. 'No.'

'Why not?'

Daniel expelled a breath. 'I guess there is no reason why I shouldn't tell you. In fact, it may help.' He paused. 'Eleanor and I married when we were both very young—

too young. She was eighteen and I was nineteen. Our parents tried to stop us, but we were in love, or so we thought, and the more they tried to stop us the more determined we were. At first we were happy. We had a flat in London and used the house in Dorset that we're going to now at weekends. My father's disapproval didn't extend to cutting me off from the family money. Not that it would have made a difference if he had. To cut a long story short, I was ambitious. Soon I was working every hour I could and only coming home late at night. I even worked weekends. Eleanor started spending more and more time in Dorset. She met someone there and asked me for a divorce. She told me she was pregnant by him, so I didn't stand in her way.'

'But Harry, he looks like you.'

A shadow crossed Daniel's face. 'That would be because he is my son. I didn't find that out until Eleanor and her new partner split. Up until then she'd led me to believe that Harry was David's child. But if I had had any doubts she was telling me the truth, the moment she showed me a picture of Harry I knew he was mine.'

That explained a hell of a lot. No wonder Daniel knew so little about his son. 'Why didn't you tell me this before?'

'I dislike talking about my personal life.'

'But this is relevant!'

'And how is my personal life relevant?'

'Because anything that affects my patient is important. I need to understand the family dynamics. It can make a huge difference to a patient's outcome.' She tried to keep the exasperation from her voice. She took a deep breath. 'Why did Eleanor wait so long to tell you Harry was yours?'

'Because she would have known I would have fought

tooth and nail to stop her leaving the country, if I'd known she was pregnant with my child. I suspect she only told me when she did, because she didn't want Harry to miss out on his inheritance.'

'So Harry didn't know you were his father until a couple of years ago?'

'No.'

'That must have been difficult—for both of you.'

'When I found out I was furious with Eleanor for keeping him away from me.' His expression darkened. 'All those years. Wasted.'

'How did Harry feel when he found out you were his father and not the man he called Dad?'

'Angry. Resentful. Mixed up, I guess. I tried to get to know him, but—' He broke off and shook his head.

'He did come to Carrington Hall to stay, though. He must have wanted to get to know you, too.'

'He came twice. Then he made excuses not to come.'

'Why did he stop?'

'I don't know. He just did. Maybe he was bored. Maybe he preferred to be in Dorset with his mother— he wouldn't say. I didn't think it was fair to make him come when he didn't want to.' His voice was casual but there was an undercurrent of something Colleen couldn't quite place. Regret? Hurt? Bewilderment?

'Didn't you miss him when he stopped coming? I mean, you could have gone to see him—or taken him out for the day.'

Daniel's hands tightened on the steering wheel and the temperature in the car dropped a couple of degrees. 'I think you're overstepping the mark, don't you?' he said finally. 'I've told you everything you need to know.'

Colleen felt her hackles rise. Why did this man make it so difficult for her to feel sympathy for him? He had been put in a difficult situation that was none of his making. But had he really tried to get to know his son?

It was another half an hour before he spoke again. 'Harry's best friend at boarding school is a boy called Nathan. You might find it helpful to talk to him about Harry. Haversham should be able to find out how to get hold of him.'

At least Daniel knew one thing about his son.

'Sounds like a good idea. Perhaps you could get Haversham on to it this morning?'

The look Daniel sent her was an indecipherable mixture of exasperation and something else she couldn't quite read. He was so different to Ciaran. With Ciaran everything was an open book and what you saw was what you got. But she knew she had got as much out of Daniel as she was going to—for the time being.

The home Harry had shared with his mother was a surprise. Given the imposing grandeur of Carrington Hall, she supposed she'd expected something similar, or, at the very least, just as grand. However, the cottage was similar to the ones they'd passed when they'd come off the motorway—a neat, compact house with a thatched roof and thick, whitewashed walls covered with roses and jasmine. Although it wasn't what Colleen had expected, the house drew her immediately.

'Does your ex-wife's husband live here now?' Colleen asked as they stepped out of the car.

'David? As far as I'm aware he's still in Buenos Aires. Mrs Hardcastle—Dora—should be here, though. The other help left after the accident, but Dora insisted on staying. She was housekeeper to my mother when I was a child and worked for Eleanor and I when we were married. She went with Eleanor and Harry to Buenos Aires and came back with them. This is the only home she knows.'

He tried the door, but it was locked.

'She's probably gone down to the village,' he said, fishing a set of keys out of his pocket. He smiled wryly. 'I can't remember when I last used these.'

Inside the house was a revelation. Unlike Carrington Hall, it was furnished in bright, welcoming colours and sunlight streamed through the windows. The door led through a small entrance hall and into a sitting room-cum-dining room. The sitting room was furnished with deep, squashy sofas in pale linen and piles of brightly covered cushions. The coffee tables were a mismatch of oak and pine and the scrubbed and dark-varnished wooden floors were covered with deep red rugs. An inglenook fireplace took up most of one side of the sitting-room wall. Just off to the right was a small but adequate kitchen and a door that Colleen guessed led up to the upstairs bedrooms.

'It's beautiful,' Colleen said. 'My idea of a dream cottage.'

Daniel was looking around, his expression bleak.

'My mother loved this house. When I was a child she used to bring me here for the summer. It was the only place that felt like home.' The last words were said so softly and with such regret that Colleen wasn't sure she had heard right. Was she seeing another chink in Daniel's armour? Maybe he wasn't so detached as he liked people to believe?

'Eleanor asked if she and Harry could live here when they came back to the UK, so I gave it to her.' Daniel continued. 'I knew Harry would be happy here.'

Colleen touched him on the arm, wanting him to

know that she understood how painful it was for him to come to the place where he had once known happiness. He looked down at her hand and his muscles tensed. She removed her hand and stepped back, feeling as if she'd been stung.

'Shall we have a look at Harry's room?' she suggested. 'See what we should take back with us?'

Harry's bedroom was the first room on the right at the top of the narrow stairs. It was small, with only just enough room for a bed, a side table and a built-in cupboard. On the table was a portable TV with a computer console attached.

'I bought him a new, bigger TV for his last birthday,' Daniel said. 'I don't see it.'

Colleen thought that a large flat-screen television would be totally out of place in this bedroom, but again decided to keep her counsel. The walls in Harry's room were decorated with posters, some from movies and others of cricketers and rugby players.

'Ah. Good lad. I see he supports Wasps. Next to the London Irish they're the best,' she said.

Daniel wandered across to the bookshelves and was looking through the books. He seemed bemused. 'I didn't know he read this! I thought he was still into Harry Potter. Isn't every kid under fifteen into Harry Potter?'

'Children move on in their tastes quite quickly,' Colleen said, keeping her voice neutral although she was dismayed. Daniel had a lot to learn about his son.

Next to Harry's bed was a bedside table. On it was a photograph of him and his mother, similar to the one Daniel had shown her. The pair had their arms wrapped around each other and were smiling into the camera. There were other photos pinned to a notice board on the wall. Photos of Harry with friends, a team photo of him with the school cricket team as well as one of him in swimming trunks holding up a cup. There was also, touchingly, an old photograph of Daniel when he must have been five or six. He'd clearly had not long finished devouring an ice cream as there were traces of the treat still clinging to his mouth and a couple of tell-tale drips on his T-shirt. An austere-looking man was holding him in his arms rigidly, as if unused to holding a child, but the little boy was looking up at the man with such devotion it made Colleen's heart ache for him.

Daniel came to stand next to her and unpinned the photo from the board. 'I remember this,' he said, his voice ragged. 'It was taken one summer when my father came to stay. He and I had spent the day looking for fossils down on Chesil Beach. It was the only day I can remember the two of us on our own just having fun. My father worked day and night at his business. He was a bit of a workaholic.' He smiled wryly. 'I guess we had that in common.'

If Daniel's father was as distant as he looked and sounded, no wonder Daniel struggled with his own child. Slowly the pieces were beginning to fall into place.

Daniel placed the photo back on the table. 'I had no idea Harry had this. There should be one of Harry and me.'

'You'll have other, good days together,' Colleen said. 'Just give it time.'

Daniel smiled tightly 'You may have gathered by now that patience isn't one of my strengths.'

There was little Colleen could say to that.

'Okay, let's pack up everything in this room.

Photographs, posters, books, his game console, even his duvet and cover.'

She started removing the posters from the wall. She had to stand on a chair to reach one that was higher up. As she stretched, the chair wobbled, but before she could fall strong arms grabbed her around the waist and lifted her off the chair. Daniel set her down on her feet and she stumbled against him. She felt the muscles of his chest against her back and his arms tightened around her. Her skin sizzled and she found herself leaning into the warmth of his body. She closed her eyes. It felt so good, so right. Unlike anything she'd ever felt with Ciaran. Horrified at the direction her thoughts were going, she stepped away.

'Oops,' she said.

She turned around to find Daniel looking at her with the strangest expression on his face. The air was suddenly filled with an almost unbearable tension. Her heart was pounding so hard she could almost hear it. Quickly she stepped away and pretended to survey the room.

'Now, what next?' she said to cover her confusion.

Harry's bed was covered in a duvet with figures from a recent movie. Colleen decided to take that, too. As she lifted the pillow to remove the matching pillow slip she found a torn-out scrap of paper from a newspaper. It was ragged around the edges, as if it had been handled many times.

She picked it up and studied the picture. It was of a man in a black gown and a wig—the kind the lawyers wore in court. Peering closer, she was startled to find that he looked very familiar.

'Who's the geezer in the wig?' she asked, handing it to Daniel.

As he took the piece of paper from her, their hands

brushed and a tingling sensation ran up her arm. Colleen snatched her hand away.

'I didn't know Harry had this,' Daniel said softly. 'Don't you recognise me?'

'Good God, that's you?'

'I'm a Q C. A Queen's Counsel. Some people call it Silk. Didn't you know?'

No she didn't know. She hadn't thought to ask Daniel what he did and just assumed he was some sort of business tycoon.

'Are you a prosecutor or a defender?'

He looked at her strangely. 'Does it matter?'

He was right. It shouldn't matter. But it did.

'I work for the prosecution,' he said after a moment.

She couldn't help but be relieved at his answer. She wanted him to be on the side of the innocent.

'But every person has the right to the best defence. In this country, people are still innocent until proven guilty.'

Damn. He was doing that reading-the-mind thing again. She felt her cheeks colour.

Daniel ran his hand through his hair. 'I handle criminal cases most of the time, but occasionally I deal with matrimonial law. Divorces, custody, that sort of thing.'

Colleen whistled under her breath. 'What kind of people have a QC represent them when they're getting divorced?'

'Very rich people,' he said, drily. He lifted an eyebrow. 'Shall we get on?'

It took them only an hour to pack up the rest of Harry's belongings. They left it at the front door for Mike to collect. Daniel was in the process of leaving a note for Mrs Hardcastle when a grey-haired woman with frizzy dark hair appeared at the door. Her lips thinned when she saw Daniel.

'Still here, then?' she said.

'This is Colleen, Dora,' Daniel said. 'She's the nurse who's going to be caring for Harry when he comes out of hospital tomorrow. Colleen, this is Dora Hardcastle. When Eleanor went abroad Dora went with her. Harry's known her all his life.'

'That child should be here with people he loves and who love him,' Dora said, pushing past Colleen and Daniel. 'Especially now he's lost his poor mother.'

'He will be with people who love him,' Daniel said. Despite his even tone, his voice had an undercurrent of steel.

'Aye, well, you say that, but he knows me best of all. He loves me. And where am I? Stuck here looking after an empty house with nothing but the memories of him and his mother to keep me company.' She pulled out one of the largest handkerchiefs Colleen had ever seen and dabbed surreptitiously at her eyes. 'If it wasn't for the fact I loved his mother like a daughter, I'd be away from here myself.'

'You know you could come and stay with us in London,' Daniel said. 'I've asked you often enough. God knows there is enough space.'

Making sure Dora wasn't looking, Colleen dug an elbow into his side. He looked at her in surprise. *Plead with her to come,* she mouthed at him.

He gentled his tone. 'We...I...would really like you to come. Please say you'll think about it.'

'And what would I be doing up there?' Dora said gruffly, but Colleen could tell from the spark in her eye that the idea appealed to her.

'You could help me look after Harry,' Colleen said.

'We could take turns sitting with him. I agree it's better for him to have as many familiar faces around him
as possible. Of course it's a lot to ask of you.'

'I know Harry looks on you as an honorary gran,
Dora,' Daniel added. 'He'd like you to be around, I'm
sure.'

Dora looked mollified. It seemed as if Daniel had hurt
her feelings when he hadn't pleaded with her to return
to Carrington Hall after the accident. Men could be so
slow sometimes.

Dora tutted and looked askance at Colleen. 'You
might be a nurse, but you don't know how Harry likes
his eggs, or how to disguise the vegetables in his food
so he'll get enough vitamins. I've been looking after
that lad since he was born. I've changed his nappies,
seen him take his first steps, fed him as a baby. I love
him as if he were my own. I hate to think of him up in
London without me.'

And she blew her nose, almost disappearing behind
her voluminous handkerchief.

'You are absolutely right, Mrs Hardcastle, I don't
know Harry's likes and dislikes. Please, please consider
coming to Carrington Hall to help,' Colleen said.

'I know it's not fair to ask you,' Daniel added, 'but
I'd really appreciate it if you would come and help look
after Harry. And I know Harry would be delighted to
have you there.'

Mrs Hardcastle's lips trembled and for a moment
Colleen thought she was going to cry. However she
sniffed and compressed her lips together. 'When is he
leaving the hospital?' she asked.

'Tomorrow.'

'In that case I'll come next week. I have some things

to organise before then. You tell the lad I'll see him soon. Now if you'll excuse me, I have dusting to do.'

Left alone with Daniel, Colleen sneaked a glance at him. He was smiling. *He should smile more often. On the other hand, maybe he shouldn't.* His smile made her feel quite dizzy.

Daniel's smile grew broader. 'Can you see Burton and Dora sharing a kitchen?' he asked.

'No. Not really.' Colleen smothered a giggle. 'I don't know how comfortable it's going to be having Dora around, but I think you did the right thing. She obviously loves Harry.'

'Anything that is good for Harry is all right with me,' Daniel said. 'Even if it means having Dora in London.' He grimaced but his eyes were sparkling. 'She and Burton don't exactly hit it off.'

'Dora doesn't entirely approve of you either, does she?'

Daniel's eyes glinted. 'That makes two of you, then, doesn't it?'

'I wouldn't say I disapprove of you,' Colleen protested.

Daniel raised a disbelieving eyebrow and her heart thumped. This man confused her. One minute she was sure she disliked him, the next he was making her heart do complicated manoeuvres. All she knew was that he was having the most peculiar effect on her.

CHAPTER SEVEN

LATER that day, back in London, Colleen surveyed the dining room, now Harry's room, with satisfaction. The heavily embossed walls were covered with posters of Harry's favourite current sport stars and a bookcase was jammed with the books they had taken from Harry's room in Dorset as well as a new selection of paperbacks from Harry's favourite science-fiction writer.

Or so his best friend, Nathan, had said. When Daniel had tracked him down, at home on holiday with his parents in Chelsea, the teenager had said he'd be glad to help Colleen get Harry's room ready. Daniel had sent Mike to pick him up as soon as he'd returned from Dorset.

Colleen was beginning to get a very clear picture of Harry in her head. At least of the child he'd been before his accident. All she was missing was an understanding of what had gone wrong between Harry and Daniel. Daniel clearly cared about his son, but the two of them seemed more like strangers than father and son. Surely two years was long enough for them to get to know each other better than they had?

'So what do you think, Nat? Will Harry like it?' Colleen had asked the serious-looking young lad.

Harry's friend had squinted a bespectacled eye. 'I think so.' He tilted his head as if he was giving the matter some serious thought. 'No, in fact I know he'll think it's cool.'

'Are you sure?' Colleen smiled. 'You don't think he'd prefer posters of the great Irish rugby players instead?'

'Nah. Definitely not. Oh, by the way, I've set up a new game on Harry's computer.' Nathan ambled over to the laptop beside the bed. 'I'll show you how it works. It's the business.'

She watched in admiration as his fingers danced across the computer keys. 'Good work, Nat. You're a star.'

Nathan smiled back, but then he wriggled about in the chair, looking as if he wanted to say something, but didn't know how to begin.

'Harry's accident must have been a terrible shock,' Colleen said, suspecting that the teen might need an opening.

'I went to see him at the hospital. A lot of us went at first. But...' Nathan bit his lip. 'Harry didn't look like himself. None of us knew what to say.'

'Try not to worry about that, Nat. A lot of people find it very difficult to spend time with someone who doesn't seem to know that they're there. But often, even if they seem to be deeply unconscious, they can hear what's being said. If Harry was at all aware, he would have been glad to hear your voice.'

Nathan brightened. 'Maybe I can come and see him when he comes home. Do you think that would be all right?'

'I think it's a great idea, Nathan. You can talk to him about all the stuff you used to talk about at school before the accident.'

Colleen went through her check list again, ticking off the items one by one. The room was ready for Harry. No doubt he would want changes, but they could be made as and when. The swimming pool was an added bonus. Colleen had already decided to get him into the water as soon as possible, but for that, she would need Daniel's help. There was no way she could do it on her own. Besides, the more involved with Harry's care Daniel was, the better—for both father and son. Now what else did she need to do?

As she set her list aside, Daniel walked into the room. Their eyes met and immediately she could tell something was bothering him by the way he ran his hand through his hair. She wondered if he knew that it was a definite tell.

'What time is the ambulance arranged for?' she asked.

'Three o'clock,' he replied. 'The doctor is coming here about five to check Harry over.'

Colleen checked her watch. 'We should leave soon.' She placed a hand on his shoulder. 'It's going to be fine, you'll see.'

Harry's transfer from the hospital had gone smoothly and a short while after being transported home by ambulance, he was safely tucked up in bed in his new room. Sometimes, when he opened his eyes, they were expressionless. At other times he would look frightened as if he had no idea where he was or what was happening to him. Daniel's presence still seemed to agitate him, so

Colleen had gently suggested Daniel leave her to get Harry settled.

'It's okay, Harry. You're in your father's house. I'm here with you and I'm going to stay until you're better.' Colleen kept repeating the words and eventually the fear would leave Harry's eyes and he would close them again. She'd seen this before. Patients would have lucid episodes where they'd seem to understand everything that was going on around them, only to have them followed by periods of confusion and apparent memory loss. Hopefully the lucid periods would increase as the days went on.

When she was sure he was sleeping, she went in search of Daniel. She found him in the library, staring down at the glass of whisky he held in his hand. He looked up and in that moment she saw such anguish in his eyes it made her wince. Then the shutters came down again, making her think of the steel doors in a bank vault slamming shut.

'How is he?' Daniel asked.

'He's sleeping. I don't want to leave him too long. I don't want him to wake up and find himself alone.'

Daniel pulled a hand through his thick hair again and frowned. 'For the first time in my life I don't know if I've made the right decision. Perhaps Harry would have been better off in a specialist unit.'

'For what it's worth, I still think you're doing exactly the right thing. You and Harry are going to have to get to know each other all over again. It will take time, but Harry will get used to you and learn that you care about him. In the meantime, he has his familiar things around him, he will have Dora, he has me and, in time, he will realise that he has you too. Nathan has promised to visit as much as he can and that will help as well. As I explained before, these next few weeks are critical.'

'I've handed over as much of my business as I could for the board and Haversham to run as I can. Unfortunately there's other stuff, upcoming court cases, that I can't pass on right now.' Daniel sketched a bow. 'Otherwise, I am completely at your and Harry's beck and call.'

Colleen found it impossible to imagine Daniel at anyone's beck and call.

'What happened to Harry's MP3 player?' Colleen asked. 'I'm assuming he had one.'

'I have it. The police recovered it from the scene of the accident and gave it to me.'

'I'd like to keep it in Harry's room so I can play it. Knowing what music he likes will be another thing it will be helpful to know about your son. If you wouldn't mind fetching it for me?'

Daniel crossed the room and pressed a button. Moments later, Burton appeared at the door.

'Ah, Burton. Could you bring me Harry's MP3 player, please? I think it's on my bedside table.'

When Burton had left the room, Daniel turned back to Colleen.

'Actually, I know what music he likes. I'm not saying I recognise it, but when Harry was in a coma I listened to it. It made me feel closer to him.' A shadow crossed his face. 'When the doctors told me that he might not survive and that I might have to think about organ donation…'

It was all Colleen could do to stop herself from going to him and wrapping her arms around him. That's what she would have done for any other relative who was in as much pain. But something held her back. For some reason, she found it difficult to behave normally towards Daniel.

Daniel shook his head as if to clear it. 'Okay, what else?'

'We're going to have to take turns being with him. I want one of us to be there all the time when he's awake. We should read to him or talk to him or listen to his music with him. He needs as much stimulation as possible and I'll need help turning him regularly. I'll be moving his limbs as much as possible to keep the muscles toned so we can get him back on his feet as soon as possible. I'm warning you, the next few weeks are going to be tough—on all of us.' She got to her feet. 'Let's continue this conversation in Harry's room. I want him to get used to the sound of our voices.'

Back in Harry's room, Colleen sat on the chair next to Harry's bed. Daniel crossed to the window and looked outside.

'No wonder Harry didn't like coming here,' Daniel said softly. 'I hated this place when I was a child.'

Harry stirred in his sleep. Colleen held her breath, wanting to know more.

'My father was a disciplinarian—almost Victorian in his view that children should neither be seen nor be heard.'

'Go on,' Colleen prompted. 'Tell me more. This is the kind of stuff you should be telling Harry when he's awake.'

'I wish Harry could've spent time in Dorset when he was younger.' He smiled ruefully. 'I wouldn't want you to think my childhood didn't have its happy moments. As I said, I used to go with my mother to the cottage at the weekends. She'd take me down to the beach and we'd do all the things families do when they're at the seaside: make sandcastles, get buried in the sand, eat ice creams. I would have done that with Harry.' He stopped speaking for a while. 'Eleanor always loved that cottage. She was a great fan of Thomas Hardy. She said it gave her a thrill to live where Tess of the d'Urbervilles was set. She always intended to write a book one day.' Daniel's shoulders were stiff. 'We were happy there.'

Something suspiciously like envy sliced through Colleen. Daniel had clearly loved Harry's mother once. Perhaps he still did. Maybe he was grieving for a missed opportunity to get back with her. She knew so little about him. *And it's none of your business. Your business is with the child and not the father.* Why, then, did she feel envious? Was it because it emphasised what she and Ciaran didn't have?

There was a long silence.

'But you didn't visit Harry in Dorset after they returned?' Colleen asked.

'Eleanor made it clear that I wasn't welcome. But, God forgive me, I could have tried harder to see Harry, but something always seemed to come up...' He turned back to Colleen and the remorse on his face made her heart twist.

'Maybe we could take Harry there when he's a little better? Stay for a while if he likes.'

In a moment the mask was back in place. 'I don't think we should take Harry back to a place that is bound to remind him that he's lost his mother.'

Colleen said nothing. Maybe he was right. It was too early yet to know what would be best for Harry. Hopefully when he was better he'd be able to tell them what he wanted.

Harry opened his eyes and blinked rapidly.

ANNE FRASER   89

'Hello, Harry,' Colleen said quietly. 'Remember me? I'm Colleen. You're back in your father's house in London. He's here, too. We've just being talking about the house in Dorset.'

Colleen waited for a reaction from Harry, but there was none. 'Now…' Colleen beckoned to Daniel '…we're just going to sit you up. Then I'll read to you. Or would you like me to put your music on?'

They helped Harry sit up in bed, Daniel holding his son against his chest while Colleen sorted the pillows.

'Okay, Harry,' Colleen said, her heart aching for Daniel. 'Blink once if you would like me to read to you.'

There was no response.

'Blink once if you would like me to put your music on.'

Again there was no response.

'Or, I can do both. I could read to you while you listen to music?'

Harry blinked twice.

'Okay, not music, not reading. What about a DVD of *Iron Man*? Your friend Nat tells me it's one of your favourite films.'

Harry blinked once.

Colleen and Daniel exchanged a look over the top of Harry's head. For the first time, Colleen saw hope in Daniel's eyes.

'Look, I need to get to the office,' Daniel said, 'but I'll be back as soon as I can.' He leaned over and kissed the top of his son's head. Harry flinched and turned his head away.

The look in Daniel's eyes changed to one of despair, but without saying anything, he straightened and left the room.

'Okay, Harry, it seems to me you can understand a

fair bit of what's going on. That's good. But just in case you forget, I'm going to keep reminding you of where you are and who I am. It might get on your nerves, but until I know for sure what you remember, I'm afraid you are going to have to put up with it.'

Colleen slipped the DVD into the slot and pressed play. 'While you're watching this, I'm going to move your arms and legs for you. It might be a bit uncomfortable, but it needs to be done if we're going to get you back on your feet. Do you understand?'

Another double blink.

'Harry, you were in a car accident. Your head got a bit of a bump. Do you remember that?'

A look of bewilderment crossed Harry's face, followed by a look of panic.

'But you're all right,' Colleen hurried to reassure him. 'Things are going to seem a little fuggy for a while, but don't try to fight it. I'm here with your dad to make sure you get better. All you have to do at the moment is let us look after you.'

The fear left the child's face and, as the DVD started, Harry fixed his eyes on the screen.

Half an hour later, he was asleep again. According to the staff at the hospital, the periods that he spent sleeping were getting shorter. If he continued to improve, sooner or later he would remember about the car accident. And then he would want to know where his mother was. It wasn't a moment she was looking forward to.

CHAPTER EIGHT

THE next few days slipped past quickly. Colleen had established a routine, knowing it was important for Harry. She got up at six and, after showering and dressing, had breakfast in her room. Then she went to Harry's room and received the report from the night nurse. Together they would wash the child and dress him before Colleen fed him his breakfast. After that she would spend the day reading to him or simply chatting to him as she put his limbs through passive movements.

After the night nurse had arrived, and Harry was settled for the night, Colleen would have a tray in her room. Some evenings she'd walk the streets of London, following her nose, delighted when she'd come across a familiar building or landmark. To her surprise, she never felt lonely. Her doubts about Ciaran were still there. Although she spoke to him every now and again, shouldn't they be talking much more often? Making plans for their wedding? Neither of them had raised the subject recently, perhaps because they were apart. Or maybe he was having his doubts, too?

Her musing was interrupted by a knock on her door.

'Mr Frobisher is asking if you would join him for dinner tonight, madam,' Burton said.

'Sure. Tell him I'll be down in a minute,' Colleen

said. To her dismay and disappointment, Daniel had been out all day for the last couple of days, only returning late at night. Often Colleen would hear his footsteps echoing in the hall and the sound of his voice murmuring to Harry. She hadn't spoken to him alone since the day Harry had come home from hospital. No doubt he wanted an update on his child's progress.

She found him in the drawing room, a glass of whisky in his hand.

'Ah, Colleen. Thank you for joining me.' He looked tired, Colleen thought. One minute she was furious with him, the next she had to restrain the impulse to touch him—to smooth his ruffled hair with her hand. She'd never met anyone who made her feel so mixed up before.

'I thought we could eat in the kitchen,' Daniel continued. He gave her a wry smile. 'If that's okay?'

'Suits me,' Colleen said. 'I was never one for formal dining.' At that moment she thought of her family—the lot of them piled around the kitchen table, all speaking at once. Up until now she had been too busy to miss them.

'Can I get you a drink?' Daniel asked.

Colleen shook her head. 'If I have any alcohol at all, I'll fall asleep.'

Daniel looked concerned. 'I'm sorry. We've been working you too hard.' He waited for her to sit, before sinking into a chair by the fire. 'I've organised the plane to take you home tomorrow for the weekend.'

Colleen covered a yawn with her hand. 'I'm not going.'

Daniel raised his eyebrows in a silent question.

'Harry is spending longer and longer periods awake. He's improving more quickly than I'd hoped,' she said.

'But that's good, isn't it?'

'Yes. But it means that he might remember the accident any day now.'

Daniel placed his glass carefully on the table and closed his eyes. 'And when he remembers the accident, he's going to ask where his mother is. God, what am I going to tell him?'

'The only thing you can tell him is the truth. He'll be upset—distraught. He might even regress a little.'

'But you'll be here?'

'He needs me,' Colleen said simply. *And you do, too,* she thought. *For all your wealth and position, there is nothing you can do to stop your child having to face the awful news that his mother is dead.*

'Thank you,' Daniel said. 'I'll make it up to you.'

'It's my job.' But that wasn't the whole of it. The truth was, despite everything she'd been taught about keeping a professional distance, she had become involved with this small, hurt family.

The clock ticked into the silence.

'I like to get Harry up every day,' Colleen said, 'even if it's just to sit. But I think he's well enough for us to try to take him out when the weather's okay. Maybe take him to a cricket match. We could all go.'

'I tried to get to his school cricket matches as much as I could. He was in the team, you know. Unfortunately I didn't get to them as often as I would have liked.'

'Work?' Colleen guessed.

If he heard the disapproval in her voice, he chose to ignore it.

'I took him to Lord's for his tenth birthday. It didn't go quite as I planned.' Daniel's smile was bleak. He took a sip of his drink. 'I wanted to spend his birthday with him. The first birthday we would spend together.

He seemed so excited when I picked him up. He barely looked at the present I'd bought him. I thought it would be a new start for us. A common interest. Something we could share.'

'Go on,' Colleen said quietly.

'I'd arranged the best seats and a picnic with all his favourite things. Eleanor had told me exactly what he liked. At first everything seemed to be going so well. He was chatting away, telling me about his matches, pointing out his favourite cricketer. And then, I don't know, something went wrong. He clammed up.'

Colleen was puzzled. 'Was it something you said?'

'I don't think so. I had guests. You know, business acquaintances I needed to speak to. It was when they arrived that Harry went all quiet. Maybe they made him shy.'

Colleen couldn't control herself any longer. 'Oh, you great big lummox of a man. Can't you see what went wrong? Here was a little boy, being taken out for a birthday treat by a father he barely knew, thinking he was going to have you all to himself—for once. Then these strangers appear and take all his father's attention. What kind of birthday treat was that for the lad?'

Daniel looked stunned by her outburst. 'I would have been happy if *my* father had taken me to a cricket match.'

Agitated, she jumped to her feet. Hadn't he listened to anything she'd said? Daniel *had* to start being more involved with his child.

'And,' she continued, 'you have to spend more time with Harry. You've hardly spent any time with him so far. I know you have your cases, but isn't it time you put Harry first?'

Under any other circumstances she might have found

the look of incredulity on Daniel's face amusing. She doubted anyone had ever spoken to him like that.

'I've changed my mind,' she said. 'I think I'll have a tray in my room if it's all the same to you. We can talk again tomorrow.'

But as she spun on her heel, Daniel's voice came from behind her.

'Colleen, wait.'

She stopped in her tracks.

When she turned around, Daniel was looking as if the demons of hell were fighting a war behind his eyes.

'When I found out that Harry was mine, I was bowled over,' he said slowly, almost as if the words were being pulled from somewhere deep inside him. 'I never thought that having a child would make me feel the way it did. Eleanor had talked about having children, of course, but only as a distant future possibility. I couldn't actually imagine ever being a father. While we were married it didn't seem there could be room for a child. When I found out Harry was mine, I was shocked—and furious with Eleanor that she'd kept him from me, but mostly I was amazed and delighted—even if I was scared to death that I wouldn't live up to Harry's expectations. I wanted to get to know my son, but what I didn't anticipate was that he wouldn't feel the same way. I didn't know it was going to be so damn difficult to talk to him.

'Taking him to a cricket match was the only way I could think of being with him. I thought that if I took it slowly—gave him time to get to know me—he'd eventually feel relaxed in my company.' He smiled ruefully. 'I can see now I made a mistake by inviting colleagues to the match.'

He pulled his hand through his hair. 'This father business doesn't exactly come easily to me.'

Colleen held her breath. She could see how hard it was for Daniel to tell her this. She sat down on the chair opposite him, mortified and ashamed by the way she'd spoken to him.

'I'm sorry,' she said. 'I shouldn't have said what I did.' And why had she? Why did she react to him instead of being able to treat him like she would normally treat any other patient's father—in a cool, caring, but professional manner?

'I like to have control in and of my life,' Daniel continued. 'But I haven't been able to control anything that's happened to Harry. Not knowing he was my son, trying to get to know him, his accident—I couldn't control any of it.' He clenched his jaw.

Colleen wanted to reach out and touch him, as if her touch could absorb some of his pain. But she instinctively knew her sympathy wouldn't be welcome.

'When Harry was desperately ill, when they thought he might die, I would have swapped my life for his in a minute. But I couldn't. I would've given everything I own in the world if that would have made him better, or brought his mother back, but for once in my life I was powerless.'

He stood up. 'Helping to get him better—that's something I can do. But I can't do it alone.'

The admission seemed to cost him the last bit of his self-control. He turned away from her.

'If you'll excuse me, Colleen, I think I'm going to do some work now.'

Colleen looked at him. He'd allowed her to see his pain. And now, more than ever, she knew she would never give up on this man and his child. She stepped across to the door and reached for the handle. She had only one more thing left to say.

'Thank you for telling me what you did, Daniel. As long as you remember that there is only one thing Harry needs from you.'

Daniel narrowed his eyes then raised a questioning brow. 'And that is…?'

'You, Daniel. Plain and simple, all he really needs is you.'

Finding it impossible to concentrate, Daniel slammed down the lid of his laptop and leaned tiredly against the back of his chair. He found his thoughts once again returning to dwell on the exchange between himself and Colleen. He stared at the closed door of the sitting room. God, what kind of harridan had he invited into his home? No one ever spoke to him like that. It was yes, Mr Frobisher and of course, Mr Frobisher. Damn it. It wasn't unreasonable to expect respect from employees, surely?

But then Colleen was a strange sort of employee. For a start, he needed her more than she needed him. But there were bound to be other nurses out there. More biddable ones for a start. Ones who wouldn't feel the need to challenge him constantly. But the truth was, he didn't want anyone else—no matter how fiery Colleen was. Harry already knew and trusted her.

And of course she had a point. Asking business acquaintances to Harry's birthday treat had been a mistake. He could see that now.

But, hell, he hadn't expected her to react the way she had. God, she certainly didn't pull her punches.

He took a gulp of his drink. He'd just told her stuff that he'd never told anyone before. Stuff that he didn't want to share. She seemed to drag it out of him. Perhaps because for some reason he wanted her to think that he was a better man than the person she believed him to be.

Which made him feel uncomfortable. Why should he care what she thought of him as long as it didn't interfere with her care of his son? He had managed all right up until now, without giving a damn for other people's opinions.

He would just have to be careful how he handled Colleen in future. One thing was for sure, he hadn't got to where he was without knowing how to get the best from the people who worked for him.

Why, then, did he have the uncomfortable feeling that in Colleen, he'd met his match?

CHAPTER NINE

A FEW days later, finding herself in the unusual position of having nothing to do as Dora was sitting with Harry, Colleen made her way down to the kitchen in search of a cup of tea. The smell of baking drifting from the kitchen made her mouth water. Although it was only a couple of hours since she'd had breakfast she was suddenly starving. Maybe she should head back upstaris while there was still time? She'd always intended to lose weight before the wedding, but somehow she only had to look at a cake and the pounds crept on. Thinking about her wedding brought back that uncomfortable feeling in the pit of her stomach.

Perhaps a slice of cake or some home-made bread would help get rid of the butterflies that seemed to have set up home in her stomach? Food always made her feel better.

Before she knew it her legs had carried her into the kitchen; to her delight, she found a freshly baked chocolate cake with lashings of fresh cream just sitting on the table begging to be eaten.

She cut three thick slices and placed them, along with a glass of milk, on a tray to take it up to Harry's room. She was still mulling things over as she made her way up the kitchen stairs, concentrating on balancing the tray of milk and cake. It was no surprise, then, that she walked headlong into Daniel who was at the top of the stairs with his mobile in his hand. Needless to say the contents of the tray went everywhere. Chocolate cake and milk in a sodden mess on the floor, but, worst of all, all over Daniel's dark-grey, once-immaculate suit.

'Oh, my God,' Colleen cried. 'I'm so sorry.' She dabbed at his jacket with a paper serviette she'd re-trieved from the floor, but that only made matters worse. Daniel looked as if he'd been in a bun fight. 'I'm such a clumsy idiot. Now you'll be late!'

Daniel was looking down in horror at his suit. Colleen waited for the explosion that was bound to come, but to her surprise he laughed.

'Hell, Colleen, do you think so little of me that you expect me to lose my cool over an accident? I'm just happy to know that Little Miss Perfect isn't so perfect after all.' His hand reached out and removed something from her cheek. 'I have to admit a little chocolate cake makes you seem more human.'

Colleen felt the colour rise in her cheeks, but then she saw the funny side of it, too. 'And I have to say, you look pretty good in chocolate cake, yourself.' There was a roar in her ears as she realised what she'd said. 'I mean—you look less severe…' Oh dear that wasn't what she meant to say either. 'I mean more…relaxed.' Maybe she should just stop talking. The problem was, or so her brothers were forever telling her, she never knew when to hold her tongue. 'It's just that sometimes you look… so scary, you frighten me, never mind Harry.'

The smile left his face. 'I frighten you? I frighten my son?' he growled. He actually growled. If he could hear himself, he would know why she found him scary.

'What I mean is, I wouldn't like to be on the opposing side to you in court. I bet you freeze witnesses with one look from those shockingly green eyes.'

He looked perplexed, but at least the gathering storm clouds on his face seemed to have gone. 'You think my eyes are shockingly green?'

Shut up, Colleen! she tried to tell the one part of herself that was still working—her brain. *Just stop talking and get the hell away from him as fast as your legs will carry you.* 'I don't mean shocking in a bad way. They're such an unusual shade of green I—one can't help looking at them.'

A small smile was playing around Daniel's mouth and those interesting green eyes crinkled at the corners. Colleen's heart was thumping against her ribs. Forget the bit about her brain working. It had packed up and gone on a permanent holiday. Was she doomed to say the wrong thing to this man?

'I take that back about you being a lawyer,' Daniel said, stepping closer to her. 'A lawyer needs to be precise. Now what exactly do you mean about my eyes?' He was so close she could make out the faint smell of toothpaste on his breath, his aftershave, his own distinct male scent. She thought if anyone was watching they would see her ribs moving from the impact of her heart beating against them. Now, she couldn't think of anything to say. The truth was, she didn't know whether she had any breath left to speak with.

At that moment Burton appeared by the door. 'Your car is waiting, sir,' he said in his sonorous voice.

Daniel smiled. 'We'll finish this conversation later,' he said to Colleen. 'I'll be back in a minute, Burton. I just have to change my suit.' And then he turned and ran upstairs, leaving Colleen wondering what had just happened.

* * *

The next morning, Colleen was with Harry in his room. She had finished putting him through the first set of passive movements of the day and was tidying up, keeping up a flow of chat to Harry, when there was a knock on the door. Daniel came in and greeted his son with a smile.

He held out a DVD. 'Look, Harry, I managed to get a copy of the 2003 rugby world cup in Australia—you know the one England won? I thought we could watch it together.'

Colleen hid a delighted smile. She wasn't sure that Daniel wasn't the one who really wanted to watch the match, but at least he'd taken her words last night to heart.

And then something happened that made her heart crash against her ribs. Harry was making a sound. It was indistinct, but he was clearly trying to speak. He hadn't spoken since the day they'd collected him from hospital. There it was again. 'Mu...'

'What is it, Harry?' she asked.

She sat down on one side of the bed while Daniel took the other.

'Mum?' This time the word was recognisable, as was the rising inflection. Clearly Harry wanted to know where his mother was. Colleen glanced at Daniel. His expression was frozen.

Daniel took his son's hand in his. 'Harry...' he started, before glancing helplessly at Colleen. She nodded at him. This was the moment they had all been dreading. But it was Daniel's place to tell Harry about his mother. She took Harry's other hand in hers and squeezed. 'Harry, your father has something to tell you. You're going to have to be very brave.'

'Mum,' Harry said again. There was no mistaking the panic in his voice.

'Harry,' Daniel started again, his voice firmer this time, 'you were in a car accident. On the way home from boarding school. Do you remember?'

There was a slight movement of Harry's head. 'No.' His voice was hoarse from lack of use. Colleen knew for certain though that he understood the question.

'Mum,' he said again. He was becoming increasingly agitated.

'Your mother was badly hurt in the same accident, Harry,' Daniel said. 'The ambulance took her to hospital. I'm afraid her injuries were too bad. She never woke up.'

Harry's eyes filled with understanding and fear. Daniel moved so that he was lying on the bed next to his son. He put his arms around his child and pulled him close. 'I'm sorry, Harry. Your mother is dead.'

Colleen ached for the misery she saw in Harry's eyes.

'No...no...no,' he said over and over. 'Mum. Want Mum.'

As Daniel's arms tightened around him, the boy struggled weakly in his arms. Harry's eyes clung to Colleen's in desperation. 'Dad go,' he said. 'Not Dad. Mum. Colleen, make him go away.'

'I think you should leave,' Colleen said to Daniel. The pain she saw in his face made her flinch. 'I'll stay with Harry.'

Daniel stumbled to his feet. Tears were rolling down Harry's cheeks. He was turning his head from side to side, still intoning the word 'no' as if he could change what he'd been told.

Daniel stood in the centre of the room as if rooted

to the spot. She could see he was torn between wanting to comfort his son and doing as Harry demanded. She stood quickly and gave Daniel a gentle shove towards the door. 'Go now,' she said. 'I'll look after Harry. I'll come and find you as soon as he settles.'

With a last despairing look at his grieving son, Daniel left them alone.

When Harry was settled and sleeping, Colleen went in search of Daniel. She looked everywhere to no avail. Finally she made her way to the kitchen. Burton might know where he was.

But to her surprise, Daniel was in the kitchen, nursing a cup of black coffee. Dora was also there, having arrived from Dorset yesterday.

'How is he?' Dora asked.

'He's sleeping now,' Colleen said. 'He was very upset. It will take time for him to get used to the idea his mother has gone. We should be prepared for some difficult days ahead.' She looked at Daniel and her heart melted. He looked so stricken, so much at a loss. His son's rejection must have cost him a great deal.

Dora got to her feet. 'I'll go and sit with him, shall I?'

'That would be good, thank you, Dora. Please call me immediately if he wakes up.'

She waited until Dora had left the room.

'Daniel…' she started, 'don't take Harry's reaction too much to heart. I—'

But before she could complete the words Daniel had jumped to his feet.

'Don't take what too much to heart, exactly? You mean I shouldn't be upset that my son can't bear the sight of me. That he probably blames me for his mother's death.' His green eyes were cold. 'And he'd be right. Is that what you want to hear? Eleanor asked me to pick him up to bring him to Dorset, but I said no. I had an important meeting.' He laughed and the mirthless sound sent a chill down Colleen's spine. 'What kind of man would put his work before his only child? If I had collected Harry as Eleanor had asked, the accident would never have happened. At the very least Harry would still have his mother.'

'Daniel.' Colleen couldn't help herself. She stepped forwards and placed a hand on his arm, but he shook her off, looking at her as if she repelled him.

'I don't want or need your sympathy,' he said roughly.

'Then for God's sake, stop blaming yourself!' Colleen retorted. 'That boy, your son, is going to need you more than ever in the coming days and weeks. He's lost his mother and he needs time to come to terms with it.' She took a breath and softened her voice. 'He's angry with the world and he's directing it at you—and can you blame him? All he has right now is a father he hardly knows. The last thing he needs is for you to withdraw.' Colleen felt her voice crack. The scene upstairs had taken its toll on her, too. Every time she thought she was beginning to understand Daniel, he did or said something that threw her. Last night Daniel had made it clear how much he cared about Harry and she didn't doubt him for a second, but he had to realise it would take Harry time to know how much Daniel loved him. She opened her mouth to apologise, but Daniel had turned on his heel.

'I'm going out,' he said and, without a glance at her, he stormed out of the room.

Later that night, after Harry was sleeping in the care of the night nurse, Colleen paced her room. She felt restless and ill at ease. She wasn't handling the situation with Daniel at all well. She was letting him rattle her time and time again. It seemed she could barely be in the room with Daniel for ten minutes and they were sparking against each other.

She opened her window and the sounds of late-night traffic and the laughter of couples returning from a night on the town drifted on the still night air. Suddenly she was almost overcome by a yearning to be back in the clear air and peace of County Wicklow.

But not with Ciaran.

The realisation chilled her. She loved Ciaran, but she wasn't *in love* with him and she couldn't marry him. Trish had been right all along. The way she felt about Ciaran was the same way she would feel if he was her brother. She felt more alive after seconds in Daniel's company than she'd ever felt in Ciaran's. Not that she was falling for Daniel. No way. No one in their right mind would fall for that pig-headed, opinionated, arrogant, interesting, exciting... *Whoa there*, she told herself, sternly. *Just because you've decided not to marry Ciaran doesn't mean you fancy another man.* Any feelings she had for Daniel were purely because she'd allowed herself to become so wrapped up in Harry—*so wrapped up in Harry and Daniel*, the voice whispered back—and their pain that she just wasn't thinking straight. But she'd never reacted to any of the other fathers like this, even when she'd been totally involved with their child.

Now she'd made up her mind she couldn't marry Ciaran, she had to let him know as soon as possible. She would have to go back to Ireland this weekend. Her heart ached for the pain she was about to cause him, but if she married him without truly loving him, that would be so much worse.

A tear trickled down her cheek and she closed the window with a decisive click. She was over-tired and over-emotional, that was all. She needed to get some sleep. Tomorrow was bound to be another difficult day. Perhaps some warm milk would help.

She pulled her dressing gown over her pyjamas, shoved her feet into her slippers and let herself out of her room. Apart from the light from Harry's night light that seeped from under his door, the house was in darkness. She popped her head around his door. He was sleeping soundly, with Sheena, the night nurse, in a chair beside his bed.

'Would you like anything from the kitchen, Sheena?' Colleen asked.

'No, thank you, love. Dora brought me some tea a little while ago.'

But instead of finding the kitchen empty, Colleen was dismayed to find Daniel sitting at the kitchen table, his long legs stretched out in front of him. He was so still that at first Colleen thought he was asleep. The kitchen was lit by a single table lamp at the far end of the room, casting Daniel's face in shadows. She was about to slip away when his voice came out of the semi-darkness.

'Couldn't sleep either?'

'I thought I'd make myself some warm milk,' Colleen said, 'but I'll leave you in peace.'

'Warm milk?' His voice was amused. 'Who still drinks warm milk?' He gestured towards her with a tumbler of amber liquid. 'Wouldn't you rather have some whisky? I find it works better.'

She wondered if he was a little drunk. At least he no longer seemed angry with her.

'No, thank you,' she said. 'Can't abide the stuff.'

'I'm sure there's some wine around here, if you'd prefer.' He waved his glass in the general direction of the room. 'Or I can ring for Burton to bring us some.'

'Don't be daft,' Colleen said. 'It's after one in the morning. Let the man have his sleep.'

Daniel's teeth flashed. 'Okay, warm milk it is.' He got to his feet and looked around the room. 'I'm sure there's a pan around here somewhere.'

'I should go,' Colleen said.

'For God's sake, woman. Stay. I'm not going to bite you. Anyway, it's me who should be more nervous than you. God knows what you're going to accuse me of next.'

'I'm sorry about earlier and the other night,' Colleen said. 'I shouldn't have snapped at you. You've enough on your plate.'

'Well, Nurse Colleen, to be honest I've had enough of people agreeing with me. It makes a pleasant change to have someone tell me what's really on their mind.'

She couldn't tell from the tone of his voice or his expression whether he was teasing her or meant what he said. She decided to take his words at face value. Otherwise there was the danger they would get into another undignified slanging match.

Daniel was opening cupboards at random, muttering under his breath when each one failed to reveal what he was looking for.

'Grief, Daniel. Don't tell me you've never cooked yourself anything in this kitchen before.' But weren't her brothers just the same? The minute they entered their mother's kitchen it was as if they lost the use of their arms and legs. Colleen took a mug from the top of the dresser where they were displayed for anyone to see.

'This and the microwave will do fine,' she said.

'Microwave? Do you think Dora would allow such a thing in her kitchen?' Daniel widened his eyes in mock dismay. Then suddenly the tension was broken.

'Sit down,' Colleen told Daniel. 'I'll do it. Would you like some, too?'

He peered at his whisky glass as if surprised to find it empty. He reached across the table and grasped the neck of the bottle sitting there. 'I think I'll stick with this if it's all the same to you.'

Colleen watched anxiously as he poured himself a hefty measure and slugged it back in one go. A sober Daniel was difficult enough to deal with, but an inebriated one? As he reached for the whisky bottle again she whisked it away. 'I think you've had enough, don't you?'

He eyed her balefully. 'Did anyone ever tell you that you're a bossy woman?'

'Many times,' Colleen said lightly. 'And I've been called worse things than that, too.'

'Can't imagine why,' Daniel said drily. He sat up in his chair. 'You know, I find myself wanting to know more about Colleen McCulloch. The woman, that is, not the nurse. That's fair, isn't it? After all, you know all my sordid little secrets.'

Colleen emptied some milk into a saucepan and placed it on the stove to heat. 'I wouldn't call your secrets sordid,' she said. 'You're no different to thousands of parents. People get caught up and fail to recognise what's important. I guess it happens to us all at some time or another.'

He leaned back in his chair. 'Letting me off the hook,

then? Somehow I can't imagine you failing to recognise what's important. Too perfect for a start.'

Her perfect? She wished! And certainly not recently. A perfect person would never have behaved towards Daniel the way she had earlier. A perfect person would never have got into the mess she had with Ciaran. A perfect person would never have become engaged simply because it seemed the easiest thing to do and their families wanted it. The truth was that was exactly what had happened and now she was going to have to do something about it and hurt someone she loved in the process. Because although she wasn't in love with Ciaran, she did care about him. No. She knew only too well she was far from perfect.

'I don't think my brothers would agree with you,' she said. 'They always claimed that Daddy let me get away with murder.'

She took her drink and sat down opposite Daniel.

'Tell me about your family,' he said. 'I'd really like to know.'

Reluctant to spoil the easy atmosphere, Colleen refrained from reminding him that he'd already looked into her family. But knowing how many siblings she had and what they did, or did not do, for a living was one thing. Knowing what it was like to be part of a noisy, argumentative but loving household, another. She could only imagine how chaotic her family would seem to Daniel if he ever met them. Which, of course, was extremely unlikely to happen.

'Mammy and Dad always owned a farm,' she said. 'At first they farmed livestock—cattle, sheep, that sort of thing—then Daddy decided that horses were the way to go. He sold off all the livestock and invested in a few brood mares. I suspect he thought that horse breeding was more lucrative somehow than cattle. He always hoped to make his fortune, you see. And that was unlikely to happen with a large family and with the prices of livestock falling all the time.'

'Were you poor?' Daniel asked.

Colleen laughed. 'That depends on what you mean by poor. I guess by your standards we were. At least in monetary terms, but in everything else, no, I always felt rich.'

'Explain,' Daniel said.

Colleen quirked an eyebrow at him. 'Is this how you cross-examine a witness?'

To his credit, Daniel looked abashed. 'Sorry. What I should have said was, "Go on, tell me more".'

'I can't remember not feeling happy as a child. At least until Cahil's accident and Daddy became depressed. But before that there was always something to do. Help Daddy on the farm or play with my bothers—when they'd let me, of course. They used to tease me about being a girl, so I was always trying to show them how tough I was. Led to a few cuts and scrapes, I can tell you.'

'Now why don't I find that hard to imagine? I can just see the little girl you were. Hair flying in the wind as you ran barefoot over the hills.'

'Come on,' Colleen retorted. 'We weren't that poor. We had shoes like everyone else.' When she saw him smile she knew she had been suckered.

'No, up until Daddy sold the cattle for the horses we were comfortably off. But somehow he could never get the hang of breeding horses.' Her heart ached as she remembered her father's slip into depression. 'I know he felt a failure, but it wasn't all his fault. One of the brood mares became unwell suddenly and had to be put down, another foaled, but her colt died. And so it went on until he was left with only one of the five he had invested in. Believe me, high-quality brood mares are expensive to buy and even more expensive to keep.

'We tried to help him, at least my older brothers did—I was too young and at school—but things got so bad that eventually my brothers had to stop helping him on the farm and find work in Dublin. My mother hated her sons leaving and my father felt it was his fault. And then Cahil had his accident. Daddy was never the same. It was as if he'd given up on life. Of course I know now that it was depression, but back then I couldn't understand why Daddy had gone from this laughing man to someone who never smiled and just sat in his chair all day long. The family kind of broke apart then. My mother was distraught. She didn't know how to help him.'

Colleen didn't know why she was telling Daniel all this. Perhaps because it was late. Perhaps it was the semi-darkness, or perhaps it was because he had been through his own kind of hell.

'I'm sorry. What happened to your brother? Can you talk about it?'

Colleen drew in a breath. 'Cahil was the youngest. I was eleven when he was born. I think he was as much of a surprise to Mammy and Daddy as he was to me. But they were happy to have another child. By that time they were still well enough off and there was plenty of room on the farm for one more. But when Cahil was eight my other brothers were working off the farm and Daddy needed help to bring one of the horses in from the field. He wasn't keeping so well by this time so Mammy suggested he wait until one of the older boys came back from work. Cahil must have been listening. He always wanted to be like the big boys. He went out to the field without telling my parents. But the horse wasn't used to him. She had a bit of a temper and was about to foal, but whatever happened we can't be sure. Mammy only noticed that Cahil was gone when she called him for his tea. They found him unconscious in the field. It looked as if the horse had reared up and kicked Cahil in the head. To cut a long story short, Cahil was in hospital for months. Mammy wanted him home. Just like you, she had no faith that the doctors and nurses would look after her baby as well as she could. Daddy was beside himself and no use. He could barely bring himself to look at Cahil. So every day after school, I helped Mammy care for Cahil. She was like a woman possessed. The doctors told her that it was unlikely that my little brother would ever be able to walk or talk or even feed himself. But she wasn't having it. She bullied and coaxed my brother and slowly he began to learn to walk and talk all over again. You should see him now. He still has some short-term memory problems and mixes up his words, but as you know he plays for the local football team and helps my mother on the farm. You would never know just by looking at him that once the doctors held out little hope.'

'So that's why you do what you do,' Daniel said. 'I knew there must be a reason why you were so driven. Your patients are just like your brother all over again, aren't they?'

She wriggled under his intense gaze, surprised by his perception.

'I guess so. I know what the power of love can achieve and that's why, no matter how much Harry pushes you away, you have to believe that right now he needs you more than ever.'

'And your father? What happened to him?'

Colleen sucked in a breath as pain lanced through her. 'He died shortly after Cahil's accident. He didn't live long enough to know that his son made an almost complete recovery. He died feeling guilty and a failure. So you see, Daniel, I know all about what guilt can do to a man.'

The clock ticked into the silence. What Colleen had said surprised Daniel. He was certain there was more to her story—his job had given him an instinct for when people weren't telling the whole truth—but if there was more, he would wait until she decided to tell him. If she ever told him. He studied her as she sipped the last of her drink. He would never have guessed that she had her own tragedy in her life. When she wasn't challenging him, hands on hips and grey eyes blazing, her mouth was curved in an almost permanent smile.

With her dark hair tumbling in loose curls over her shoulders instead of clasped back in the usual ponytail, she looked younger, less severe. Her skin was pale, almost translucent, with an alluring sprinkling of freckles across the bridge of her nose that he found unbearably cute. In fact, there was a great deal about Colleen that he found cute. He liked the way her grey eyes sparked when she was in a temper. He liked the way her mouth twitched when she was trying not to laugh. He liked the way she stood up to him, he liked the way she treated his son and he even liked the way she looked, even in those ridiculous bunny slippers she was wearing on her feet and those childish pyjamas. Her dressing gown had fallen open slightly, revealing a spaghetti top, exposing creamy shoulders and just a hint of cleavage. On the bottom half she was wearing boxer shorts depicting cartoon characters. His brain saw all this, registered it logically and coolly, but there was nothing cool about the way his body was reacting. He hadn't seen her legs before—they were usually hidden by the trousers she always wore, but who in their right mind would hide legs like that? They were slim and toned. The sort of legs that just begged a man to run his hands up their silky smoothness. When she'd leaned over him to place his milk on the table in front of him he'd caught a scent of vanilla and strawberries and he'd shifted in his chair to hide his sudden and immediate response to her. Perhaps it was the whisky or perhaps it was because he'd not been with a woman for a long time? But suddenly an image of Colleen lying underneath him, her body all sweet curves and softness, her grey eyes clouded with desire, filled his head. He shook the image away.

Maybe he was seeing her in a different light because she had allowed him to see the vulnerable side of her.

No wonder he was rattled. The last thing he'd expected was that he couldn't get the Irish harridan out of his head. She was nothing like the women he usually dated. All of a sudden he wanted to see her at one of the dinners he attended—the looks on the other women's faces as she outshone them with her simple beauty despite their designer dresses and hundred-pound haircuts. He bit back a groan. Great. That was all he needed right now. A developing case of the hots for his son's nurse—a woman who just happened to be in love with another man.

CHAPTER TEN

COLLEEN stretched languorously as the sun poured in her bedroom window. For some reason this morning, she felt happier than she had since she took up the job here. She smiled to herself. Maybe it was because she had come to a decision about Ciaran and because some of the tension between her and Daniel had disappeared. After all, her job would be so much easier without the constant clashing of wills. Or maybe it was because she had talked to Daniel about her dad? No one in the family could bring themselves to talk about those final days. Not in front of their mother anyway. They were all too scared that a mention of his name would send Mammy into another paroxysm of grieving. Perhaps it was time that they did talk about Daddy? When she was home next she would try.

She jumped out of bed before Dora could arrive with her tea. She couldn't get used to being served her tea in bed by the housekeeper. It seemed so lazy.

By the time she came out of the shower the tea tray had been left on the table. Dora had even added a small vase of flowers. It seemed that Dora was beginning to thaw towards her. But when she bent to pour the tea, she noticed a small envelope addressed to her in unfamiliar handwriting.

Puzzled, she tore it open. It was from Daniel. It was brief and to the point. 'Thanks for the warm milk. And for telling me about your brother. Most of all thank you for caring about my son.'

Something shifted behind her ribs. Daniel wasn't so bad once you got to know him. They had got off on the wrong foot, that was all. And if her heart had done a crazy little pirouette when she'd seen the note was from him, well, that was just a sign of the pleasure she felt that they seemed to have reached an understanding.

As soon as she was dressed she went to Harry's room. After their chat last night, she'd half-expected to find Daniel by his son's bedside and not just the night nurse. Colleen tried to ignore the thud of disappointment—which was, of course, on behalf of Harry, wasn't it?

'Morning, sunshine,' she chirped.

Harry turned his head at the sound of her voice and smiled. Colleen felt her heart melt—what would happen the day that devastating grin finally reached his emerald eyes? Then she'd be a goner, that was for sure. She was getting far too fond of Harry already, but there was something so special about this young man that she couldn't help herself.

The night nurse gave Colleen a quick handover before she left. 'Has Mr Frobisher been in to see Harry this morning?' Colleen asked softly, so that Harry couldn't hear.

The nurse—Sheena—nodded. 'An hour ago. Harry was still asleep. Mr Frobisher didn't stay long, though, said he'd an important meeting to go to and wouldn't be back till later.'

Colleen closed the door behind Sheena. So much for thinking she'd got through to Daniel last night. It was all she could do to stop herself from marching to the nearest telephone and telling Daniel Frobisher exactly what she thought of him! But she had Harry to concentrate on and that was far more important. Instead, she pulled open the curtains and flung the patio doors wide before turning back to her charge.

'Oh, Harry, it's such a beautiful day—too good for staying indoors. Are you up for some fresh air?'

Harry nodded his head slowly and moved his mouth. 'Yes. Outside. Nice.'

Colleen laughed in delight. 'Excellent, Harry—you're doing it! You're almost there—before you know it you'll be chatting twenty to the dozen, giving me a run for my money, eh?'

His grin widened and Colleen put her hands on her hips in mock horror. 'Are you trying to say I talk too much, young man?'

A sound of delight bubbled from Harry. It was the nearest she'd seen him come to laughing properly. Oh, why wasn't Daniel here to see his son take these tiny, but oh-so-significant steps forwards? Despite his protestations of love, words, after all, were easy to say— acts of love were much harder to do. If only he could understand how much he was missing out on.

She tilted her head to the side. 'You know, Harry, I think you're ready to try something new this morning.' Suddenly his eyes widened in fear and his smile faded. Colleen sat on his bed and reached for his hands, stroking them gently. 'No, no, don't worry. Trust me, Harry. I won't do anything to harm or frighten you, you know that, don't you?'

When Harry didn't reply, she continued, keeping her

tone light and soothing. 'Your dad told me how much you used to love swimming, especially when you were little. Well, I think we should try swimming today; it will really help your arms and legs rebuild their muscles. What do you think?'

Still he gazed back at her. 'I know you're not sure about it, Harry, but I promise I'll look after you. You'll be safe with me, you know that, don't you, sweetheart?'

Harry nodded slowly.

Colleen didn't want to let him see how relieved she felt. If he'd refused or become agitated, there was no way she could have forced him. It was vital that Harry trusted her completely so that he would feel safe in the water and hydrotherapy would bring on his mobility in leaps and bounds. Colleen ruffled his har. 'You're my trooper, aren't you? A brave young man, that's what you are! And it'll be fun, you'll see.' With expert practice she dressed him in a pair of boxer shorts and, using the hoist, manoeuvred him into his wheelchair, chatting all the while. Despite her best jokes and quips, Harry didn't smile once. Colleen could sense his apprehension.

She knelt down in front of him. 'I know you're still unsure, Harry, so I'll tell you what. Will it make you feel better if I ask Burton to help?' Colleen grinned. 'Hey, maybe I should ask him to put on a costume and come swimming with us. He might have one of those one-piece bathing suits that goes to his knees.'

She was rewarded with a smile. Now all she had to do was persuade Burton!

'You wait there, now. Give me a minute while I put my costume on and give Burton the good news.'

To give him credit, Burton didn't put up as much resistance as she'd expected. Perhaps he was too used to

Daniel's extravagant requests that nothing much fazed him any more—not that she could imagine what those would be. Who knew how the rich and priviliged lived?

Still, she felt a bit guilty laughing at him behind his back. But it had been worth it to have made Harry smile, she thought.

To her surprise, Burton was already there waiting for them and she almost pushed the wheelchair into one of the elaborate marble columns when she saw him. What in all that was holy was he wearing! Far from the old-fashioned costume she'd half-expected, the older man was dressed in the skimpiest briefs she'd ever seen in her entire life. If he'd worn a wig and a false moustache, she couldn't have been more taken aback.

Colleen averted her eyes from his expanse of bare chest and hairy back, although it took a huge amount of will power to keep her gaze from straying away from his. It was as if her eyes had a sudden will of their own. Thank God they had to concentrate on getting the hoist round Harry and lowering him on to the sling at the side of the pool. When he was secure, Colleen slipped into the warm water and between them they lowered Harry in.

Whilst Burton sat on the side, Colleen slipped her arms under Harry's back and eased him free. His eyes cast round desperately and she tilted him towards her, so that he could see her face.

'Well done,' she soothed. 'I've got you and I'm going to let you go, Harry. Just try to let the water swirl around you.'

It took a fair amount of cajoling and encouragement, but within ten minutes she felt her young patient begin to relax. 'You're doing really well, sweetheart.'

Suddenly she noticed his gaze slip from hers to over

her shoulder and he tensed. Colleen turned round in the water so she could see what had caught his attention.

It wasn't what—it was who. Daniel stood uncertainly at the side of the pool. Thankfully he didn't shop in the same store that Buton did and his swimming shorts were far more modest. She couldn't help noticing that they somehow accentuated his tanned, smooth chest and broad shoulders and didn't make his muscular legs look too shabby either.

'Can I join you?' Daniel asked.

'What do you think, Harry? Can your dad swim with us?' Colleen gazed down at the young lad, willing him to relax. She looked up and caught Daniel's eye. Almost imperceptibly, she nodded.

Daniel nodded to Burton. 'That's okay, Burton, I'll take over from here.'

'Very well, sir.' There was no mistaking the look of relief in Burton's eyes. Colleen caught Daniel's eyes and for a moment his lips twitched. Clearly he found the sight of Burton in his swimwear as amusing as she did. Colleen's heart skipped a beat.

With a graceful ease belying his size, Daniel dived in at the deep end and swam towards them. Harry's eyes widened and he flailed his body, pressing himself as close as possible to her. The arm around her neck tightened and his fingers grasped her hair. Ignoring the sharp pain, Colleen kept her tone even. 'Remember when I said you could trust me, darling? Remember when I promised I wouldn't let any harm come to you? Well, it's the same with your daddy. He only wants to help, Harry.'

Harry tore his eyes away from his father and looked at her. His deep-green eyes searched her face, looking for the slightest hint that she wasn't telling the truth, and in that moment she knew that if Daniel let him down now, made one wrong move, the tiny delicate thread holding father and son together would be broken—maybe forever.

'How about letting your dad hold you? That way I could move your arms and legs about a bit in the water?'

'No.' Harry shook his head.

Colleen met Daniel's gaze over Harry's blond curls. His anguish was unmistakable, but yet he didn't move away from them.

She brushed her lips against Harry's cheeks. 'Your dad is a big strong man, darling, and he's going to hold on to you tight.'

Finally Daniel spoke. 'I won't let you go, son. I promise you.'

Gently Colleen untangled Harry's arms from around her neck and eased him towards his father. Between the two of them they held the too thin child, until Colleen felt his under-used muscles finally relax.

Signalling to Daniel with a nod of her head, she again reassured Harry, 'I'm going to let go now, but just so I can move your legs, okay? Your dad's got you safe.'

As Colleen moved away, Daniel eased himself down into the shallow water, cradling his son in his arms. She watched as, ever so slowly, Harry's arms snaked around his father's neck and clasped on to him tightly.

For a split second she could see Daniel's eyes widen in surprise, then he was looking down at his son, beaming from ear to ear. Pulling him closer, until his blond curls were tucked into his neck, Daniel looked at Colleen.

Thank you, he mouthed.

'What would you like to do this afternoon, Harry?' Colleen asked a couple of days later. 'I know Nathan is coming over this morning, but if the weather clears up later, perhaps we could go out for a while?'

As they were talking, Dora came in with Harry's breakfast and set the tray on the table.

'I think you should have a go at feeding yourself,' Colleen said to Harry. 'Now you're bound to make an almighty mess at first, so we'll do it before your wash. How about it? Are you willing to have a go?'

Colleen cut up Harry's toast that had been supplied with his scrambled egg into easily manageable slices. She wouldn't call them soldiers. Harry would hate to be treated as if he were five instead of twelve.

To her delight, Harry managed, although with some difficulty, to pick up one of the pieces of toast in his hand and bring it towards his mouth. She waited with bated breath as he concentrated hard on bringing the morsel to his lips. Finally, after a couple of false starts, he managed to get it in his mouth. The fine motor control required meant that he was improving in leaps and bounds. He was making progress far quicker than she had dared to hope.

Just as they had finished breakfast and Harry was sitting up in his chair by the window, Daniel came into the room. He was wearing dark trousers and an open neck shirt—no tie.

'Hello, everyone,' he said. 'I've taken the morning off work so we can spend it together. What would you like to do, Harry?'

Harry glanced up at his father and smiled briefly.

'Nathan,' he mumbled.

'Nathan's coming this morning,' Colleen said quickly, seeing Daniel's disappointment. 'What about doing something this afternoon instead? I was just saying to

Harry that we should try to have a session in the pool, but we could all go somewhere later.'

Daniel ruffled Harry's hair.

'You could have Nathan over another day,' Daniel said. 'I have to be in court this afternoon. It would give us the chance to do something together first. And you can choose.'

The boy pulled his head away and Colleen caught the bleak look in Daniel's eyes before the usual mask came down. *Don't push it*, she wanted to say. *Give him time.*

Harry shook his head again. 'Nathan!'

Daniel's mouth tightened. 'You can have Nathan visit later. I've taken the morning off, despite the fact that I should be going over this afternoon's case, so I think you and I should do something this morning, Harry.'

Harry flung Colleen a look so full of entreaty she couldn't ignore it. Daniel was going about this all wrong. Couldn't he see that?

'I think since Nathan is already coming over, we should leave things the way they are,' Colleen said evenly.

Daniel pulled a hand through his hair and a look of resignation crossed his face. 'Whatever you prefer, son.' And with one final look at Colleen, he turned on his heel and left the room.

Harry looked angry. As well he might be. 'Dad. Work. Typical,' he said. 'No time for me.'

Although Colleen was thrilled that Harry's speech and understanding was so much improved, it was the relationship between father and son that was concerning her.

'To be fair to him, Harry, he didn't know Nathan was expected. Your dad did want to spend time with you.'

She crouched by Harry's side and took his hand. 'You need to be patient with him. He's trying his best.'

But Harry pulled his hand away. 'You on his side.'

'I'm not. If anything I'm on yours. But I know your father loves you. He's just not sure how to show it.'

She reached out and gently turned Harry's face towards her, forcing him to look in her eyes.

'Give him time, darling.'

Suddenly tears were rolling down Harry's cheeks and he buried his head in Colleen's chest. 'Want…my… mum,' he said between sobs.

'Oh, sweetheart, I know you do.' And Colleen's heart cracked as she held the sobbing child.

After Nathan arrived, Colleen left the boys playing a computer game. Nathan was working the controls, but Harry seemed to be engaged with the game, offering 'yes' and 'no's at regular intervals and even an 'idiot' once.

She tapped on the door of Daniel's study and marched in without waiting for an invitation.

Daniel looked up from his papers and frowned. 'Now's not a good time, Colleen,' he said roughly.

'It seems that there's never a good time, Daniel,' she said. 'Have you any idea how upset Harry is?' She was furious. Despite what she'd said to Harry about giving his father time, how much time did he need? After everything they had spoken about, Daniel still didn't have the faintest idea how to go about building a relationship with his son.

'If you think that the occasional visit with him, or the odd DVD, is going to cut it, then you're a bigger fool than I thought.'

'Harry—' Daniel started, but Colleen stopped him with a wave of her hand.

'Your son is making progress—fantastic progress. But do I need to remind you that he has just lost his mother. He loved his mother deeply and that little boy is *grieving*. And not only has he lost his mother, but he's lost the only home he ever really knew. He's lost the ability to play cricket, to play computer games, he can only express himself with great difficulty and he's only just learning how to feed himself.'

'He's managing to feed himself? But that's great.'

'Please don't interrupt me, Daniel. Yes, it's great that he's learning to do that. But it's not so great that he's having to learn to do everything he once took for granted all over again. Your son has shown, *is* showing, great strength of character, God knows he must have got if from his mother—but every day is a struggle for him. What he needs now, most of all, is to know that he is the most important person in your life. That you are with him literally every step of the way. That you will love him, even if he doesn't improve from where he is now. He needs to know that he can count on you. His father. The person who will be there for him through thick and thin and never ever let him go no matter what happens.'

The shell-shocked look on Daniel's face had slowly turned to anger. 'I don't like to be lectured, Colleen. I am making time for him. If I could be with him all the time, don't you think I would? But there is a small matter of my job.'

'Of course. Your job!'

'Yes, my work. When I heard about the accident I was in the middle of the biggest court case of my life. Do you think that mattered to me when my son was seriously ill in hospital and his mother was dead? But believe it or not, no matter what terrible personal tragedies are happening in people's lives, the world continues. People who need you to act for them don't care what's going on in your life, not when they could be sent down for years because they weren't represented properly. I managed to get the case deferred for a while, so I could spend time with Harry in hospital, and then when it was clear that he was going to be there for some time, I tried to hand the case on to a colleague. But the client wouldn't have it. Funnily enough, he trusted me. He believed, rightly or wrongly, that I was the only person who could save his neck, and he was right. I am bloody good at what I do. It's his case that is starting this afternoon—the preliminary hearing—and I should be in chambers as we speak, going over the defence reports one more time, but because my son needs me, I am here. I can't be with him this afternoon, and not very much over the next few weeks, certainly not as much as I would like to be, but I have no choice.'

His breath was coming in short rapid bursts as if the effort of keeping himself under control was costing him dearly. Colleen was stunned by the naked pain in his eyes.

'So why didn't you just tell him that? Explain? The way you have just explained to me? Your son is angry, hurting and not just physically, but he loves you and I suspect from the photograph we found under his pillow—he's proud of you. At the moment he thinks you're not giving him the time or attention he craves, because you're not interested. Tell him the truth. Spend every minute you're not in court, or preparing, with him. Even if it's just sitting with him.' An idea was forming in her head. 'And maybe—I don't even know if this is possible…maybe I could bring him to court some time so he can watch you.'

They were both staring at each other across Daniel's desk. For a moment there was a silence. Something seemed to shimmer in the room. Colleen's heart was pounding so hard she could almost feel it kicking against her ribs. Daniel reached across and tucked a lock of her hair behind her ear.

'Has anyone ever told you, Colleen McCulloch, that you're some woman? Anyone would be lucky to have you on their side and fighting for them. Maybe you should have considered a career in the court?'

Colleen's legs felt as if they were about to give way. She reached behind her for the chair and almost collapsed into it. Why was everything with this man so… fraught?

Daniel leaned back and studied her through half-closed eyes as if she were a problem he couldn't quite get a fix on. 'I'd like Harry to come to court one day. Perhaps then he'll understand why it was so difficult for me to be around.'

'If you want him there so you can excuse your absence from his life, then I think it's going to take much more than that.'

'Determined not to let me off the hook?'

Colleen used the edge of the desk to ease herself on to still-weak legs.

'I think it's you that has to let yourself off the hook, don't you?' And with as much grace as she could manage on her wobbly legs, she left the room.

CHAPTER ELEVEN

DANIEL was still feeling irritable when he got up the next morning. As soon as he was dressed he crept into Harry's room to say goodbye before leaving for chambers. The night nurse rose from her chair as he entered the room, but he signalled for her to stay seated and crossed over to Harry's bed. His son was still sleeping, his blond hair, so much like his mother's, falling across his brow.

Harry sighed in his sleep and Daniel's chest tightened. Why hadn't he tried harder to get to know his son when he had the chance? He could still have been a lawyer and made a decent living without working almost every waking hour. The money had never really interested him.

Haversham had been handling most of his father's business since Harry's accident and was doing a good job. Realistically, all Daniel needed to do was attend the monthly meetings and study the published accounts. His court cases were another matter, especially the *pro bono* ones. If he didn't take them on, who else would?

He bent down and kissed Harry on the cheek before saying goodbye to the nurse and letting himself out of the room. Who was he kidding? He worked because the truth was he didn't know who Daniel Frobisher was outside work. Doing what he did defined him. But yesterday, spending time away from the never-ending cases piled up on his desk hadn't prevented his cases from being as well prepared as they should be. But if he were honest with himself—and with Colleen around to be his conscience, it was hard to be anything else—he did find spending time with his son difficult. He didn't have a clue how to reach him—how to talk to him, how to simply be with him—not the way Colleen, a comparative stranger, did. But she was wrong about one thing. He would never give up trying to learn how to be the kind of father Harry deserved. Perhaps there was a way to spend time with his son while keeping on top of his cases. Surely all he had to do was work harder?

CHAPTER TWELVE

THE following day Daniel woke up with a smile on his face. He couldn't remember when he'd looked forward to a day off before. In fact, when had he last taken a day off? When had he last gone to the theatre? Or to a concert or even for a drive? Haversham was dealing with the business and Daniel wasn't due in court until tomorrow. From now on things would be different. He would spend proper time with his son, do all the stuff he should have done years ago. The stuff that according to Colleen other fathers did with their children. Starting today. Yesterday in the pool when Harry had clung to him he'd felt as if his heart would break. Up until now he wasn't even sure that he had one to break. It had felt good to hold Harry in his arms. And that was down to Colleen. For the first time he allowed himself to believe that his son would come back to him. Maybe even learn to love him.

The rain had disappeared and the sun was streaming in the window. He would ask Colleen where she thought they should go today. He jumped out of bed and into the shower. Thinking of Colleen made him smile. This house with its large, empty rooms had never felt like home before. Now he found himself listening out for light footsteps on the wooden floors, the sound of her laughter. God, he even liked it when she was confronting him, hands on hips, eyes blazing with indignation. And those hips. He'd noticed them before when she'd come down to the kitchen and he couldn't help notice them again when he saw her in the pool. And it wasn't just her hips. It was her tiny waist and her small but perfect breasts. With her long hair plastered to her face she looked like some sea sprite just risen from the sea. God, she was bringing out the poet in him, too. He was even beginning to think in the same rhythms that she spoke.

As soon as he was dressed, he went to look in on Harry. His son was still sleeping, his light blond hair falling over his forehead and his mouth only beginning to lose its childish softness.

Daniel closed the door gently on his sleeping son and bounded downstairs to the kitchen. He sneaked up on Dora, who was busy stirring a pot on the stove, and wrapped his arms around her waist.

Dora shrieked and spun around.

'Mr Frobisher! I didn't hear you coming in. What's with the boyish pranks? Aren't you getting too old to be frightening an old lady half out of her wits?'

Daniel grabbed a piece of toast from the kitchen table. 'Sorry, didn't mean to frighten you. I just felt like giving you a hug.'

Dora eyed him speculatively. 'What's brought all this on? I haven't seen you look this cheerful for a long time. Far too long a time.'

Daniel sat down on the kitchen chair. 'For the first time, Dora, I believe that Harry's going to be okay. Really okay. How can I not be happy about that?'

'I heard he's turned a corner. Colleen was down here

not a minute or two before you, telling me all about it.'
Dora's eyes grew soft. 'I'm so happy for you. That girl
seems to know what she's doing.'

'You mean Colleen?' Daniel said casually. 'I always
knew she was the right person for Harry.'

'And the right person for you, perhaps?'

Daniel jumped to his feet. That was going too far.
'Sorry, Dora. You know I'm never going to get married
again. I was rubbish at it when I was married to Eleanor
and I'm never going to put another woman through that
again. Apart from that, don't you know Colleen is getting married herself? In a couple of months' time, if I
remember.'

'So she told me,' Dora said, drily. 'Anyway, what are
you wanting for your breakfast? The usual glass of orange juice to go with your toast. Bacon? Eggs?'

'The full works, Dora,' Daniel replied cheerfully.
'I've a feeling I'm going to need some fortifying for the
day ahead. Then I'm going to take Harry's breakfast up
to him.'

Once he'd eaten Daniel went back to Harry's room with
a tray. His son was sitting up in bed and managed a
small smile when he saw his father. It was still nothing
in comparison to the smiles he bestowed on Colleen,
but it was a start. 'What about breakfast?' he asked.
'Porridge and toast?'

Harry pulled a face.

Daniel laughed. 'Okay, maybe we can hide the por-
ridge from Colleen. But let's give the toast a try.' He
turned to the night nurse. 'I can take it from here. You
might as well get off.'

'I don't like to. Not until Colleen gets here.'

Daniel looked at his watch. It was still early. 'I doubt

she'll be here for another half an hour or so. Don't worry, we can manage, can't we, son?'

To his relief, Harry nodded.

After the night nurse had said her goodbyes and left, Daniel buttered Harry's toast and cut it into small pieces. 'My mother used to do this for me when I was a little boy.'

Tears welled in Harry's eyes. 'Mum used to,' he said.

Daniel's chest tightened. His first instinct was to pretend he hadn't heard. But he could almost hear Colleen's voice telling him that he had to find the words to comfort his son.

'Your mother loved you very much,' Daniel said. 'When my mother died, I was too young to really know that she wasn't coming back. Sometimes I'd want my mum so bad, I thought I would break into pieces. I was angry with her for not coming when I needed her.'

Harry's eyes were fixed on his face. Daniel struggled for the right words. God, he wished Colleen was here. She'd find exactly the right words. He lay down on the bed and put his arm around his son.

'Dora was our housekeeper back then. She told me that my mother would always be part of me. That she was watching over me and that she wouldn't want me to be sad or angry.' His throat was so dry he could barely speak. 'It wasn't always easy to remember that, but I tried to and it helped.' He smoothed Harry's hair with his hand. 'I know that your mother would never have left you if she had the choice and that she is somewhere watching over you—even if it's because of the memories you have of her inside.'

His words sounded so inadequate. He glanced at Harry. Although he looked unconvinced, his eyes had cleared. If only Daniel had tried harder to get to know his son, perhaps he would have found the right words. But there was no point in thinking about what could have been—should have been—he had to deal with the present.

'Hear her in my head,' Harry said. Although the words were slurred, it was the first complete sentence Daniel had heard his son say. The tightness in his chest eased. He was beginning to see a future—not just for his son, but for them together.

When he'd finished helping Harry with his breakfast Daniel slipped a DVD into the player. 'I thought we could watch the match we didn't see the end of the other day. Would you like that?'

'Work?' Harry said.

'Not today, Harry. I plan to spend the whole day with you.' A small smile crossed his son's lips.

They had been watching the match in companion-able silence when Colleen came into the room.

'Well, look at the pair of you,' she said, pretending to be cross, 'Watching TV before breakfast.'

'We've already had it.' Daniel nodded his head to-wards the empty bowl. He'd flushed most of the por-ridge down the toilet. Not that he would tell Colleen that. 'We're looking forward to when we can have a burger.'

Harry's face lit up. Then he said 'Yes. Burger.' As before, although it was indistinct the meaning was clear.

'I think it's time we asked the speech therapist to come, guys,' Colleen said, looking delighted. 'With her help we'll have you chatting away in no time.'

She picked up the tray. 'I'll leave you two to it,' she said, 'while I have my breakfast. But as the sun's shin-ing, what do you say about going out to get some fresh air this morning?'

'Sounds good to me.' Daniel winked at Harry. 'Take your time with breakfast, Colleen, so we can see the end of the match, eh?'

By the time Colleen returned, however, the sunshine had turned to heavy rain and a trip outside was out of the question. But now that Harry was making progress she wanted to establish a more normal routine. Keeping him in his room all day had never been part of the plan. Dora was sitting in the chair by the window, knitting as she and Daniel chatted.

'Time to get dressed, Harry,' Colleen said.

Harry looked at his father. 'Not Dad. You and Dora.'

Colleen was delighted. Harry's speech was coming on so quickly now that she suspected it was only a matter of time before he was speaking more or less normally.

'Why don't we let Dad go and check his emails while Dora and I get you dressed?' she suggested. Harry was at that age where he'd feel uncomfortable having his father dress him.

Luckily, Daniel seemed to catch on and excused himself. 'I'll be back in twenty minutes. Maybe the rain will have gone by then.'

When Daniel left. Harry scrabbled at his bedclothes. It looked as if he was trying to get out of bed.

'What is it, Harry? What do you want?' Colleen asked.

'Walk.'

Dora and Colleen shared a glance.

'You want to try walking?'

Harry nodded.

'Tell you what, why don't we have you sitting at the side of the bed while we get you dressed? Then we can see how you manage to stand. Your muscles are going to be weak at first, so you might only manage a minute or two at first, but that and the swimming is a good way of getting some strength back in your legs. What do you say?'

They got him dressed in his jeans and a T-shirt, Colleen and Dora taking turns to thread his arms through the sleeves.

'Why don't we stand you up while we pull your jeans up?'

They took Harry's weight between them while Colleen pulled up his jeans and fastened them.

'Okay. Try to take as much of your own weight as you can. Dora and I will be here to catch you if you think you're going to fall.'

Very slowly they decreased their support until Harry was standing. It only lasted a few seconds before he swayed and had to be helped back into his position at the edge of the bed.

'That was fantastic, Harry! Well done. We'll keep trying. But you'll see, soon we'll have you back on your feet and maybe then you can try a few steps. How does that sound?'

Harry grinned up at them. 'Good.' Then he shook his head. 'Don't...Dad.'

'You don't want me to tell your dad, Harry. Is that what you're trying to say?'

Harry nodded.

'But he'll be thrilled. He's been so worried about you.'

Harry's expression settled into one Colleen knew very well. It was the same one she'd seen on his father's face several times before. It seemed the son was as stubborn as the father. But in terms of Harry's progress that was good. Harry would need all his stubbornness and determination in the weeks and months to come.

'Fair enough, sweetie. If you don't want me to tell your father, I won't. From now on it's up to you to keep him up to date with your progress. Unless, of course, something happens and I have to tell him. Deal?'

Harry's smile was back.

'Deal,' he said.

Daniel had quickly dealt with his emails before returning to Harry's room.

'The sun's shining again so I thought the three of us could go out somewhere. Does anyone have any preferences? Of course you're welcome to come too, Dora.'

'Funny, Harry and I were thinking just the same thing. Harry would like to go to Hyde Park, if that would be okay?' Colleen said.

It was uncanny how Colleen seemed able to communicate with Harry even with Harry's speech being so limited. Daniel had seen it happen too often not to know that it was genuine. She would ask a question and, depending on Harry's yes or no, ask another until she had established what Harry wanted. Over the time she'd been here, their unique form of shorthand was developing to a point where she seemed to know what Harry wanted with very little difficulty.

'I'll stay here if that's all the same to you,' Dora said. 'My legs aren't what they used to be.'

As they were about to leave the doorbell rang. Daniel opened it to find a man with longish dark hair and a cheerful smile.

'Hello,' the stranger said in an Irish accent. 'Is Colleen about, by any chance?'

'Ciaran! What on earth are you doing here?' Colleen said, from behind Daniel. 'Not that it isn't good to see you,' she added hastily.

Was it his imagination or did Colleen seem less than enthralled to see her fiancé? The thought cheered Daniel immensely.

He watched Colleen lift her face for Ciaran's kiss. So this was the man she loved? This unremarkable individual with his bad haircut and washed-out jeans was the man Colleen was intending to marry? He simply couldn't see it.

'I thought, if you couldn't come to see me, I would come to see you, Col,' Ciaran said.

Col? What kind of name was that? It didn't suit her.

Ciaran pulled Colleen into his arms and hugged her.

Colleen returned the hug half-heartedly. She glanced at Daniel and flushed, before wriggling out of Ciaran's embrace. She turned to Harry, who had been watching them with interest.

'Harry, this is my fiancé, Ciaran. Remember I told you about him?'

Harry nodded and with a huge effort lifted his hand from his lap and held it out towards Ciaran.

Ciaran took it and shook it. 'Col's told me a lot about you, Harry. It's grand to meet you at last. She tells me you're a rugby fan. Well, so am I.'

Colleen looked at Daniel, delight written all over her face, and he grinned back. Harry's movements were becoming more and more purposeful.

Then she frowned. 'I'm sorry, Ciaran, but now's not a good time. We're about to go out to the park. Where are you staying? Perhaps we can meet up later?' She looked at Daniel for confirmation.

He nodded reluctantly. After all, Colleen was entitled to time off. He had no right to stop her seeing her fiancé. Even if the thought made him feel…resentful was the word that came to mind.

'I came straight here,' Ciaran said. 'I thought there might be a B&B nearby.'

'You are welcome to stay at Carrington Hall,' Daniel found himself saying. He didn't want Ciaran staying here. In fact, he wanted him a thousand miles away. But he couldn't *not* ask him. There were seven empty bedrooms in the house. The very least he owed Colleen was to make her fiancé welcome. Even if it was the last thing he wanted.

'Oh, Ciaran will be happy with a B & B,' Colleen said, quickly. 'Isn't there one nearby?'

Of course—Colleen and her fiancé would want to have somewhere they could meet in private. Daniel ignored the knot in his stomach

'If that's what you'd prefer, of course,' he said, 'I'll ask Burton to arrange it.' He signalled to Burton, who nodded and picked up the telephone.

'There is a decent establishment a couple of streets away, sir. I'll give them a call now.'

'And of course you should have the day off. Harry and I will manage on our own,' Daniel said.

But as he glanced at his son he saw a stricken look cross his face. Obviously, despite the improvement in their relationship, Harry wasn't ready to be alone with him. The buoyant feeling he'd had when he'd woken up was fast disappearing.

Colleen must have seen Harry's reaction too, as she quickly crouched beside Harry and took his hand. 'What? And miss Harry's first trip out? No way. Ciaran won't mind waiting until we get back, will you?'

'Or I could come with you,' the idiot said, cheerfully. 'It's not as if I've got anything else to do—'

'I'm not sure Harry should be introduced to new people at this stage,' Daniel interrupted. 'It's perfectly all right if you just want it to be the three of us, Harry. I'm sure Ciaran will be happy staying behind. He's probably tired.'

'Oh, I think if Harry's fine with Ciaran coming, then that's okay. Harry would tell me if he didn't want him along. Wouldn't you, sweetie?'

Harry smiled and nodded.

'The Duchess Hotel has a room available, sir,' Burton said. He turned to Ciaran. 'It's just a short walk from here, sir, but I could ask Mike to take you.'

'Why don't I walk with you as far as my hotel?' Ciaran said. 'Col, we could meet there when you've had your walk.'

Could that be relief on Colleen's face? No, that was wishful thinking on his part. No doubt she preferred to see Ciaran alone away from prying eyes.

With the decision made that Ciaran would accompany them as far as his hotel, the four of them set off. Colleen insisted on pushing Harry. As the pavement was too narrow for the three of them to walk side by side, Daniel found himself alongside Ciaran.

'Did you fly?' he asked.

'Just jumped on a plane at Dublin this morning. Luckily there was space. If there hadn't have been, I would have taken the ferry.'

'You should have said. I would have sent my plane for you.'

'I wanted to surprise Col. She's looking grand, isn't she?'

Daniel followed Ciaran's gaze. Colleen's ponytail was swinging as she walked and her bottom undulated deliciously with every step she took. Daniel bit back the groan that rose to his lips.

What exactly did Ciaran expect him to say? *Yes, she's*

looking good. She looked even better in her bikini. In fact, I think she's quite beautiful. She has a smile that lights up a room.

'Yes. She has a great deal of energy.' Good God, couldn't he have thought of something else to say?

Ciaran laughed. 'You can say that again. Col's never happy unless she's bustling around and has plenty to do. The only time I see her sitting still is when she has her nose in a book. She's been like that as long as I can remember.'

'How long have you known her?' Daniel asked, his curiosity piqued.

'Since she was about ten. I was—am—pals with her older brothers. She was always a bit of a tomboy.' Ciaran frowned. 'Is she okay? I mean, she sounded a bit strange the last time I spoke to her on the phone.'

'She seems all right to me,' Daniel replied.

Daniel was pleased when Ciaran peeled off at his hotel. Thankfully there was no repeat of the earlier hug. Colleen simply gave Ciaran a wave and, as Daniel took over chair-pushing duty, she fell into step beside them.

It felt odd to be out like this, almost as if the three of them were a family. Which was ridiculous. Harry was all the family he wanted or needed.

The park was mobbed with people, riding bikes, picnicking and generally relaxing in the first real sunshine of the month. Daniel caught a badly aimed frisbee as it came his way and returned it, and was pleased to see it went in the general direction he'd planned.

'Is there anything you'd like to do in particular, Harry?' he asked. But to his dismay his son's expression had darkened and he turned his face away from him.

Quickly Colleen crouched by the side of Harry's chair. 'I know it's tough, Harry, seeing all these people doing stuff you used to do. But you've got to believe me when I tell you that I really believe that in time you'll be able to do more—a lot more. There's no reason why you might not be able to throw a frisbee yourself. Do anything you put your mind to, in fact.'

Perhaps this hadn't been such a good idea after all. All it was doing was reminding Harry of what he could no longer do. Harry pointed over Colleen's shoulder. Daniel had been so intent on keeping an eye on the frisbee throwers that he hadn't noticed another group playing cricket. Suddenly he saw something fly towards the air directly towards Harry. Before he was even aware of what he was doing he had thrown himself forwards just in time to catch the missile in his right hand. However, his impetus threw him on to the ground where he landed in an untidy heap.

Feeling an idiot, he was about to jump back up when suddenly Colleen was there, leaning over him, anxiety flooding her grey eyes.

'Are you okay? Speak to me, Daniel.'

He no longer felt the need to move. It was kind of nice to have Colleen bending over him. She bent lower to peer in his eyes and as she did so her ponytail fell forwards, enveloping him in the smell of strawberries and vanilla. He groaned.

'What have you hurt? Can you sit up?'

He considered laying it on a bit thicker, but decided against it. They had Harry to think about. He grinned at her and jumped to his feet. He looked down at his hand. He was still holding the missile, which turned out to be a cricket ball. If that had hit Harry, God only knew what damage it would have done. He turned towards his son. Harry was smiling.

'Good catch, Dad,' he said.

Colleen looked at Ciaran across the table and took a deep breath. 'I have something to tell you, Ciaran,' she said. She hadn't expected Ciaran to jump on a plane and come and see her. But now he was here, she had to tell him.

For once Ciaran looked serious. 'I think I know what it is.'

'You do?'

'Come on, Col, we've known each other for ever. You've never been any good at keeping things hidden from me. You've decided not to marry me. Am I right?'

'I am so sorry, Ciaran.' She reached a hand across the table and Ciaran took it. 'How did you guess?'

Ciaran smiled sadly. 'It's been this way for a while, hasn't it? I've known for months you were having your doubts, but I thought if I said nothing, things would just get better. Anyway, it's not just you whose been having doubts. I love you, Col, you know I do, but I've met someone recently and she looks at me the way someone who's in love with you is supposed to look at you. The way you and Daniel look at each other—as if you have stars in your eyes.'

What on earth did he mean? If only Ciaran knew how often she and Daniel argued.

'That's nonsense, Ciaran. I sometimes think Daniel would like nothing more than to give me a good shake and as for the way I feel about him...'

'You're in love with him. Anyone with a pair of eyes in his head can see that.'

'In love with Daniel?' Had Ciaran completely lost the plot? 'No way.'

'And he's in love with you. I knew it the moment I saw the way he looks at you.'

'You're got it completely wrong, Ciaran. Daniel and I can barely be in the room together for two minutes before sparks start to fly.'

Ciaran leaned back in his chair. 'Exactly,' he said.

Colleen's head was spinning. Was Ciaran right? Could this crazy feeling in the pit of her stomach, this urge to be around Daniel, this feeling as if every nerve ending was tingling whenever he was around, be love? If so, it didn't make her feel good. It made her feel awful.

No, of course she wasn't in love with Daniel. It was just that she'd never met anyone like him—someone who made her feel more alive than she ever had before. But that wasn't love. That was lust. And as for him being in love with her? Hah! Nothing was less likely.

'You've got it all wrong, Ciaran. But I'm glad you're okay about us not getting married.' She smiled back at him. The relief of breaking off her engagement and knowing Ciaran wasn't upset, made her feel lighter than she had in days.

She twisted the ring from her finger and handed it to him.

'I hope we can still be friends.'

'Hey, we're breaking off our engagement, not falling out. Of course we'll always be friends, Col. And I will always love you—and your crazy family. You know that, don't you?'

She returned his grin. 'So tell me about this woman who looks at you with stars in her eyes, Ciaran. I want to know everything.'

CHAPTER THIRTEEN

Daniel let Burton take his jacket. It had been another tough day in court, but he was confident they would get the verdict they were seeking. In a day or two the trial would be over and he could take time off to be with Harry. He had cleared his diary, refusing to take any more cases for at least four weeks. Harry would have his undivided attention during that time.

'The doctor is here to see you, sir,' Burton said.

Daniel's heart thudded. Had Harry relapsed? Handing his briefcase to Burton, he hurried into his son's room. The doctor was leaning over Harry, listening to his chest.

'Hello, Dad,' Harry said.

Daniel's chest felt tight. 'Hello, son.'

The doctor straightened. 'Your son is doing well,' he said. 'His speech is pretty much back to normal and, despite a continuing weakness in his right side, it looks like he's making excellent progress.'

'What do you think of our star boy, then?' Colleen said, her grey eyes sparkling.

'I think he's amazing,' Daniel said. He perched on the side of Harry's bed and ruffled his hair.

'Not a baby, Dad,' Harry said.

The doctor packed his stethoscope away in his bag. 'You should have a rest, Harry. You've had a busy day. Although you're improving, don't try and do too much too soon.'

'We've been in the pool again this morning,' Colleen added. 'Nathan and Burton helped.'

Guilt coiled in Daniel's chest. He should be the one helping his child. But over the coming weeks he'd be able to do just that.

'I have a couple of days more in court, son,' Daniel said. 'But after that, I'm on holiday. We can go into the pool every day and maybe you and I could go to a cricket match?'

Harry looked at Colleen, anxiety darkening his green eyes. Daniel felt the look like a blow to his solar plexus.

'Don't worry, Harry. I'm not going anywhere,' Colleen said quickly. 'Not until you're ready.'

'I think I want to sleep now,' Harry said.

Daniel stepped outside with the doctor, leaving Colleen to settle Harry.

'Will he make a full recovery?'

'It's too early to say how much he'll continue to improve, but, yes, if you all carry on doing what you're doing, I see no reason why your son won't be able to return to school after the summer. He may still require a wheelchair, but that in itself shouldn't prevent him. I am warning you, however, that he may experience some lack of concentration and some mood swings for some time yet, so be prepared.'

Mood swings and a loss of concentration were nothing compared to the prospect of having his son permanently disabled. His decision to seek out Colleen had been the right one. Perhaps his son would have improved anyway, but he couldn't help but believe his rapid progress was at least partly down to Colleen.

Daniel had waited outside until Colleen emerged, closing the door gently behind her.

She looked up at him and smiled. He loved her smile. It made it seem as if there were a thousand candles burning behind her eyes.

'He'll sleep for a couple of hours. I told him to press his buzzer when he wakes up.'

'I don't know how to thank you,' Daniel said.

'All in a day's work,' Colleen said breezily.

'Don't be modest, Colleen,' Daniel said. 'It doesn't suit you. I know what Harry and I owe you; if there's anything I can do to thank you, you only have to say the word.'

'I'm being thanked well enough,' she said. 'You already pay me three times the going rate.'

'That's not what I meant.'

Colleen looked at him with her steady grey eyes. A man could happily drown in those eyes. How come he'd never noticed before?

'It's enough,' she said. 'It's great, though, that you've taken time off. We can get Harry into the pool every day. We can take him places—to see you in court—to a cricket match—anywhere he fancies.'

'Perhaps we could go somewhere this weekend?' Daniel suggested.

'You could go anywhere you like, but I'd like to go home this weekend. There are things I need to get sorted.'

A strange feeling coiled in Daniel's chest. He didn't want Colleen to go home—even for a weekend.

'I'd prefer it if you could stay this weekend.'

'I'm sorry. I would like to, but…' She tailed off. 'I really need to go home. I wouldn't ask to go if it wasn't important.'

Of course, she wanted to see her fiancé. The thought gave him no pleasure. He especially didn't want to think of her with Ciaran. But he had no right to try to stop her.

Just then Dora appeared with a tray. 'I have some sandwiches and cake. Where would you like it?'

'No more cake.' Colleen groaned. 'Another couple of weeks of your baking and I won't be able to fit into anything.'

'There's nothing wrong with the way you look,' Daniel protested. 'Nothing at all.'

To his delight, Colleen blushed. She was the only woman he knew that did. And it only made her more appealing to him. He'd choose Colleen McCulloch with her what-you-see-is-what-you-get manner over the superficially glamorous women he usually dated, any time.

'You can always use the gym downstairs,' Dora suggested. 'Seeing as someone has spent a fortune on it.'

'I hate the gym. It's like a medieval form of torture,' Colleen replied with a smile. 'But I may well be forced to give it a go.'

'We'll take tea in the garden,' Daniel said. 'Please join me, Colleen. I could do with not having to think about my case for a couple of hours.'

'I don't suppose one little sandwich will hurt,' Colleen replied. 'And I was planning to take my book into the garden to read. If we sit near Harry's room, we can hear him when he wakes up.'

Daniel took the tray from Dora. He knew he should ask the older woman to join them, but this was too good an opportunity to get Colleen to himself for a while. So they could talk about Harry, of course.

The wrought-iron table and chairs were only a short distance from Harry's room and Daniel set down the tray and sat down.

'It's a beautiful day,' Colleen said, picking up the bone china teapot. 'I hope the weather stays like this for a while. How do you like your tea?'

'Like my coffee. Black,' Daniel replied and watched her through half-closed eyes as she poured the tea. She took a satisfied sip and closed her eyes, turning her face to the sun. 'I wonder what they're doing back in Ireland,' she said. 'No…wait…I know what they'll be doing. Ciaran will be seeing to the horses with my brothers. Mammy will be in the kitchen, making dinner with the dogs at her feet.'

'Do you miss them?' Daniel asked.

'I've never really been away from them for very long. I spend all my days off on the farm.'

'I gather you've known Ciaran a long time.'

'Since for ever, it seems. We were in high school together. He was friends with my oldest brother and used to hang about the farm. I can hardly remember a time when I didn't know him.' His chest tightened when some of the light went out of her grey eyes.

'Do you love him?' The question surprised even him.

'Actually, Daniel, Ciaran and I have broken up. The other day—when he came to London.'

A wave of delight surged through Daniel. But why was she looking so sad?

'Was it Ciaran who broke it off?' If it was Ciaran and Colleen still loved him, that would account for the look in her eyes. His delight faded.

'I'd really rather not discuss it, Daniel.'

That wasn't good enough. He had to know how she felt.

'Mum! Mum!' The panicked cry came from Harry's room and Colleen and Daniel were on their feet and running. 'Colleen!'

They burst into Harry's room. The boy was struggling to sit up, a look of terror on his face. 'Where's Mum?' he cried. 'I want her. Please, Colleen, I need her.'

Daniel was across the room and gathered his son into his arms, cradling the sobbing child against his chest.

'Shh, Harry. It's okay. I'm here. Dad's here.' He looked at Colleen for support. God, how often would this happen? Colleen didn't move. Daniel continued to hold his son until the sobs quietened to only the occasional hiccups.

'Mum. She's dead, isn't she?' Harry said. 'I keep dreaming she's here next to me.'

'She is next to you. She might be dead, Harry, but she's looking over you from wherever she is. But I'm here.'

'Don't leave me, Daddy,' Harry said.

Daniel hugged Harry tighter. 'I'm never going to leave you, son. Not ever.'

Colleen had left Daniel comforting his son. She could have intervened, but it was Daniel that Harry ultimately needed. The sight of Daniel holding the son who looked so much like him made her heart twist. It would take time before the rift between them was completely healed, but if Daniel would keep his promise it was a start. It wouldn't be long now before she could go home and leave this small family to get on with their lives. The thought made her heart ache even more. Damn it! Hadn't she promised herself that she wouldn't get overly emotionally involved with them? She was here to do a job and if that job was nearly done, she should be happy and not filled with dismay.

She went upstairs to change for dinner. As the evening was warm she would swap her usual jeans and T-shirt for a summer dress. She also decided to let her hair down. Peering at her reflection in the mirror, she was irked to see that there were shadows under her eyes. Maybe she should do as Dora suggested and spend some time in the gym? She'd spent so much time inside with Harry lately; no doubt all she needed was some fresh air and exercise.

She found Daniel and Harry, who was sitting up in bed, watching a DVD. Although Harry wasn't looking at Daniel, neither was he turning his head away.

'Hello, you two,' Colleen said. 'What are you up to?'

'It's the test match between England and Pakistan. It's almost finished. Do you want to watch it with us?'

'Don't understand the first thing about the game. Now if you were watching a rugby match that would be different.'

'Not like cricket? Is she nuts, do you think, Harry?'

A small but unmistakable smile crossed Harry's mouth. It seemed that more than physical progress was being made. Although his eyes were red rimmed, he seemed more settled than she'd seen him for a while.

'Look, I've had an idea,' Colleen said 'I'm going home this weekend. But why don't you both come too? One of our dogs has just had a litter of puppies and I'm sure you'd like to see them, Harry. You can also meet my brother Cahil. He had a head injury a few years ago and you might find it helpful to meet him. He'll know exactly what you are going through. What do you say?'

The idea had just come to her, but the more she

thought about it, the more it seemed like a plan. She could see her family and be able to keep on top of Harry's therapy.

A broad smile crossed Harry's face. 'Puppies! Could we have one, Dad?'

'If Colleen can part with one, I don't see why not.' Daniel frowned and looked thoughtful. 'But Harry and I couldn't put your mother out. Doesn't she have a pretty full house as it is?'

'Oh, Mammy can always fit in another couple of bodies. She loves having people to stay and she'd love to fuss over Harry. Now her children are all almost grown up, she's always asking when any of us are going to have kids so she can have children about the farm again.'

A shadow crossed Daniel's face as if something she had said displeased him. Perhaps the thought of roughing it was a step too far? After all, this man was used to having a whole house to himself. He was more used to five-star hotels than a crowded farmhouse. 'But...' she went on hastily, 'please don't feel you have to come.'

'I want to go,' Harry said. 'Please, Dad. I want to see the horses and the puppies.' He looked anxious. 'I want to stay with Colleen.'

It was only natural that the child didn't want to be separated from her. He had got used to her being around. But as his relationship with his father improved, he'd need to become less reliant on her. If Daniel was upset that Harry didn't seem keen to have him on his own for the weekend, he gave no indication of it.

'If you're sure your mother won't mind a couple of extra guests, then we'd like to come,' he said. 'We could take the plane on Friday and come back on Sunday evening.'

'That's settled, then,' Colleen said. 'I'll let Mammy know. Now, why don't we all have dinner together?'

After dinner when Harry was back in bed and Daniel reading to him from one of the books they had brought back from Dorset, Colleen had phoned her mother to let her know there would be two extra guests at the weekend. She'd already told her that Ciaran and she had broken up, but her mother hadn't seemed the least bit surprised. The phone call finished, Colleen let herself out of the door and into the garden. Although it was eight, the sun was still up. Harry had managed to feed himself pretty well after Colleen had cut up his food for him. It was another step in the right direction.

'Can I join you?' Daniel's deep voice came from behind her. Her heart thumped.

'Sure. I was just about to go exploring. Is Harry asleep?'

'Yes. Why don't we walk this way?' Daniel took her elbow and an odd zinging sensation shot up her arm.

'I want to thank you again,' he said. 'You've made such a difference to Harry and in such a short time.'

'He's a determined boy. Takes after his father, I suspect.'

'Why don't you ever take a compliment when it's given to you?'

'I'm happy to accept compliments any time,' Colleen said. Annoyingly, she sounded breathless as if she'd been on a gallop on one of the horses.

'In that case, you should know that you look beautiful tonight.' His voice was easy, almost teasing, but there was an unmistakable undercurrent in his words. Was it possible Daniel Frobisher was flirting with her? Had Ciaran been right when he said Daniel was attracted to her? She immediately dismissed the thought. Daniel's words were just the well-oiled ones of a man used to charming people.

Daniel reached across and touched her gently on the cheek. 'Do you know two dimples appear just here when you smile?'

The touch of his fingers made it difficult for her to breathe. Okay, so he was definitely flirting.

'Have you kissed the Blarney stone recently?' she asked, striving to keep her voice light.

He laughed. She liked it when he laughed. It made his face soften and his green eyes glint. Good God, what was she thinking? And her just recently unengaged? It wasn't as if she and Daniel had anything in common—apart from Harry, of course.

'Maybe you *should* be a lawyer. You always have a ready answer. I'm going to miss you when you leave.'

She felt a pang of loss at his words. The faint scent of his aftershave drifted on the still evening air.

'I won't be leaving for a while,' she said. Again she felt that hollow sensation in the pit of her stomach. One day she would be back in Ireland, her time here a distant dream.

'What's wrong, Colleen?' he asked. 'Are you okay?'

She shook her head. 'Now what could be wrong? My patient is getting better. His father is taking time off to be with him. Soon I won't be needed here.'

'Harry will miss you terribly,' Daniel said. 'And so will I. We've got used to having you around.'

Used to having her around. Like a friend. Her heart sank. Maybe it was because she was tired. She didn't want Daniel to be her friend. It felt unsatisfactory, yet... dangerous.

'I'm tired,' she said. 'If you don't mind, I think I'll turn in for the night.'

Suddenly his hand was in her hair and he leant down and kissed her lightly on the lips. For a moment the world spun. 'Good night then, Colleen. I'll see you in the morning.'

After a night spent more awake than asleep, Colleen gave up trying to sleep and slipped out of bed. She glanced at her watch. It was only six. Too early to wake Harry. She supposed she could go for a walk, but it was raining hard outside.

But she needed to get rid of this restless feeling somehow. Making up her mind, she pulled on a pair of shorts and a T-shirt and headed down to the gym. Exercise would help.

The gym had weights, which she ignored, a treadmill and another machine Colleen hadn't seen before. She decided that half an hour on the treadmill would do the trick. If only she could remember how to use it. The last time she'd been to the gym was with Trish a couple of years ago. But how difficult could it be?

There was a quick-start button so Colleen pressed that. The treadmill started to roll beneath her at a rapid–but-doable walking speed. This was okay.

But then, to her consternation, the running machine started to speed up. She broke into a jog, but the machine kept increasing speed until she was practically sprinting. She glanced around frantically for a stop button, but before she could reach it, she stumbled and, before she knew it, the machine had thrown her off as if it were a badly behaved horse.

She lay in a crumpled heap on the floor, wondering what had just happened and trying to get her breath back.

'Are you having a nap down there?' an amused voice came from above her.

She looked up to find Daniel looking down at her, grinning. Slowly her eyes travelled down from his face. He was wearing a sleeveless T-shirt that emphasised the muscles in his arms and a pair of low-slung tracksuit bottoms. What little breath she had caught in her throat. She closed her eyes as her cheeks burned.

He crouched next to her. 'Normally people stay on the machine,' he said.

'Very funny,' she gasped. Hopefully he'd put her shortness of breath down to being on the machine. She struggled into a sitting position. 'I don't know what happened. One minute I was going along just fine. The next the damn thing was trying to make me do a seven-minute mile.'

'It's programmed to go to twelve mph after a two-minute warm-up,' Daniel said. 'That's the setting I always use. You needed to set it manually for your speed.'

His jade eyes were alight with mirth.

'You might have told me,' she said huffily.

'I would have, had you asked. Did you hurt yourself?' His hands were on her ankles, gently pressing.

A flash of heat ran up Colleen's legs all the way to her pelvis. 'I'm fine,' she said.

'Hey, relax. Let me just make sure.'

She closed her eyes and tried to ignore the way her body was overheating from the touch of his deft fingers on her skin. What was the matter with her? How could her body be responding this way? It had never behaved like this when Ciaran had touched her.

'Everything seems in one piece.' His voice sounded hoarse.

Colleen forced her eyes open. He was looking at

her intensely. Their gazes locked and Colleen's breath stopped in her throat.

He placed his hands under her arms and pulled her to her feet. He held her against him for a long moment. She became aware of the heat of his skin burning her fingertips before he muttered something under his breath and released her so abruptly, she staggered a little. Or was it because her knees were weak?

'I'll set the treadmill for you,' he said, 'at a more appropriate speed.'

All Colleen wanted to do was to escape to her room so she could examine these strange sensations coursing through her body. 'No, you obviously wanted to use it.'

'I was going to lift some weights,' Daniel said. 'I can do that while you're on the machine.' He was punching something into the buttons on the front of the machine. Colleen had no choice but to step back on and, with her knees still feeling as if they were made from plasticine, started running at a more sedate pace.

As the equipment was in front of the running machine, she was forced to watch as Daniel lay down on a bench and started lifting weights.

The way his muscles contracted and bunched every time he raised the weights above his chest did nothing to help the warm feeling in Colleen's abdomen.

After fifteen minutes of her trying to concentrate on keeping her wobbly legs moving, Daniel stood up and pressed a switch. The treadmill slowed to a stop.

'I think that's long enough for your first day.'

'I was managing fine,' Colleen protested. 'I could have gone on for twice as long.'

Daniel smiled at her and, if she hadn't known it was impossible, her heart rate went up another twenty beats.

'It's better to mix your work-out routine,' he said. 'A bit of cardiovascular with a bit of resistance training.'

Resistance training was just what she needed, but not the kind he was referring to.

'Come on. I'll help you lift some weights,' he said.

Unable to find enough breath to refuse, she let him lead her over to the bench he had been lying on.

She lay down on the bench with her legs draped over the end.

Daniel placed a bar with weights on either side in her hands and stood behind her.

'Okay, now lift them straight up,' he said.

She did as he instructed.

'That's good, but don't lock your elbows.' She felt his hands on her elbows. 'Keep a little bend here.'

There was no way she could do this. If he continued to touch her the way he was doing, she would start to whimper. She placed the bar back in its holder, looked at her watch and faked dismay. 'Goodness. Is that the time? I must go. I want to have a shower, then it'll be time for the night nurse to leave and I don't want to keep her waiting.'

She sprang to her feet, only too aware of his amused eyes on her.

'Thanks…er…for your help. I'll see you later?' And before he could say anything, she flicked her fingers at him and, as casually as she could manage on legs that felt like rubber, walked out of the room.

Daniel watched Colleen's retreating back until she'd disappeared. He reset the treadmill to its usual setting and started to run. He would do an extra five miles this morning, he decided. He needed something to distract his head—and his pelvis—from the image of Colleen in her skimpy shorts and T-shirt. He felt a smile tug at his mouth. What was it about her that drew him? It wasn't just that he found her so sexy, it was the way he felt good around her. She captivated him in a way no woman had before. He never quite knew what she was going to do next and he found himself constantly listening out for the sound of her voice, her laughter, her quick steps.

He turned the speed up and ran faster.

Dear God, it wasn't just that he had the hots for her— somewhere along the way, he had fallen in love with her. And no amount of telling himself otherwise was going to make the slightest difference.

CHAPTER FOURTEEN

THE flight to Dublin was short and uneventful. They hadn't had to queue at security. All they had to do was show their passports and then they were ushered on to the plane. Daniel had carried his son up the short flight of steps as if he weighed no more than a bag of sugar. The three of them had played 'Go Fish' during the flight—after explaining the rules to a baffled-looking Daniel. She hadn't seen much of him since that day in the gym, and when she did, he had treated her with his usual courtesy. She'd almost managed to make herself believe that she was mistaken about the charged atmosphere between them.

'I win,' said Harry, waving his empty hand in the air. 'You're useless at this, Dad.'

'Just as well I don't have to make my living as a card player, then,' he laughed. He looked good in his short-sleeved, open-necked shirt and jeans. Almost too good.

And he and Harry were getting on well, although Harry would tell his father off every now and again for babying him.

The journey to the farm had taken an hour and Colleen had felt herself relax as soon as Daniel had steered the car off the motorway and on to the country roads leading to the farm. Her mother had cleared out one of the unused farmworker cottages for Daniel and was planning to put Harry into Colleen's old room as it was the only one on the ground floor.

As soon as they stepped out of the car Colleen's mother came rushing up to greet them. 'I've put the dogs away in case they jumped on Harry,' she said. As soon as Daniel had transferred Harry to his wheelchair, she bent down and shook Harry's hand. 'I'm Sheila, Colleen's Mammy. You must be Harry. Welcome to our home.'

Harry smiled shyly. 'Thank you for asking me.'

Sheila straightened. 'And you must be Harry's dad. Daniel, isn't it? Well, come in, Danny and Harry. Let's get you fed. Colleen tells me you're wanting to see the puppies. We'll do that after you've had a taste of my special dumplings. Why don't you go and say hello to your brothers, Colleen, while I settle our guests?' She waved a hand in the direction of the hills. 'They're out there somewhere.'

'It's okay, Mammy. I'll catch up with them later. I want to be around when Harry sees the puppies. Actually, I can't wait to see them myself.'

The large, scrubbed pine table in the kitchen was laid for tea. There were plates groaning with sandwiches, others piled high with home baking, while her mother's enormous tea pot took centre stage. It was always like this, Colleen thought, happily. The minute she stepped inside this room it was as if she'd never been away.

Daniel pushed Harry in his wheelchair up to the kitchen table and Colleen handed the sandwiches around. It was an inspired choice by her mother as Harry would be able to feed himself. If she'd made soup, he would have needed help. Colleen knew instinctively that the lad would have hated that in front of people who were strangers.

'Do you like horses, Harry?' Sheila asked.

'Yes. I can't ride, though.'

'Colleen could take you up on Dobbin if you like. He's as gentle as a lamb and my daughter rides better than most people can run.'

Daniel stopped eating and stared at Colleen in surprise.

'I'm a woman of many talents,' she quipped.

'Why? What else can you do?' Daniel said with a wink at Harry.

Colleen pretended to think. 'Mmm. Let me see... I can do a Sudoku puzzle in under three minutes and I'm an okay pool player. Learnt from my brothers.'

'Don't let her fool you, Daniel. She wipes the floor with most of the men down at our local.'

'We should have a game some time,' Daniel said.

Colleen smiled and shrugged nonchalantly. 'Sure, as long as you don't mind losing.'

The look he gave her left her in no doubt that that wasn't going to happen—not in his lifetime at any rate. Or was she reading too much into his lingering gaze that was oh so difficult to pull away from. Flustered, Colleen pushed her chair back from the table. 'Leave the dishes, Mammy, I'll do them. You sit down and relax for a bit.'

Sheila looked incredulous. 'What do I need to relax for? Besides, wouldn't it be good if you showed our guests to their rooms?'

Colleen knew there was no point arguing with her mother. 'Let's get Harry settled first, then.' With a tilt of her head, she beckoned Daniel to follow her and Harry down the hall.

'Harry's in my old room,' she said over her shoulder.

'It's got French doors leading out to the back courtyard as you can see.' The three of them squeezed into the small bedroom and Colleen coloured at the poster of a once-popular Irish boy band on the wall.

Harry looked at Colleen and grinned. 'You didn't like them, did you?'

'Hey, they're Irish. Of course I love them.'

'Seems the more we find out about Colleen, the more she surprises us!' Daniel said. The gleam in his eyes made her heart lurch.

'Can we go look at the puppies now?' Harry asked. 'I want to choose the one that's going to be mine.'

'Of course we can.' Anything to get away from Daniel and that breath-stealing look in his eyes. 'Then we'll show your dad his room.'

Daniel looked around the tiny bedroom of the cottage where he'd be staying for the next couple of days. He lay down on the narrow bed. If he stretched his arms out wide he could touch both of the walls simultaneously and if he stretched out to his full height, his feet would touch that wall, too. Come to think of it, it was very like the room he'd had in boarding school. That had been about the same size and was equally sparsely furnished. But this room didn't fill him with dread as that room had. This room was bright and, with the addition of a vase of wild flowers on the bedside table, more welcoming than most rooms in which he had stayed in the past. The whole house had the same sort of feel. The McCullochs weren't rich, anyone could see that, but what they might be lacking in wall-to-wall TVs was more than made up for by the warm and friendly atmosphere.

And Colleen was at the centre. Just as she was at the

centre of his and Harry's life. And he didn't want her just because he needed her—he wanted her because he couldn't imagine a life without her. Now she was no longer engaged, it was time for him to find out whether she could love him.

Leaving his unpacking for later, he went to find her.

Colleen was pushing Harry in his wheelchair towards him.

'Are you coming to see the puppies, Dad?' Harry said excitedly. Already his son seemed happier than Daniel had ever seen him. Although he needed time alone with Colleen, it would have to wait for a few minutes. Soon, he hoped, they'd have all the time in the world.

The puppies, who were in a small enclosure in one of the other, unused outhouses, were, as Colleen had guessed, an instant hit. Harry watched in delight as the chocolate Labradors squirmed and wriggled over their mum in an attempt to feed. He was far more delighted with the puppies than any present Daniel had ever given him. Once again, Colleen was right. Harry wanted company and attention, not gifts. How come he hadn't been able to see that before?

But he knew the answer. He hadn't known it before because he had needed Colleen to show him what love meant.

'They're only small yet,' Colleen told Harry, 'so you won't be able to take one home for another couple of weeks. You can choose one today though, if you like. She reached out for the biggest puppy and placed it in Harry's lap. What about this one? He has the cutest white socks.'

Harry petted the puppy for a few moments before pointing to the littlest one who was struggling in vain to shove his brothers and sisters out of the way so he could feed, too. 'I want that one.'

Colleen looked doubtful. The puppy Harry had pointed to was the runt of the litter and so small it was possible it might not make it.

'Won't you prefer one of the others? That little one isn't doing so well.'

But Harry stuck out his lower lip. 'That's why I want him. He's weak, like me. But he's going to get better, get stronger, like me.'

'If that's the one you want, that's the one you're going to have,' Daniel said firmly. If he and Harry were about to lose Colleen, this was the least he could do to make it up to his son.

Not that he was ready to let Colleen walk out of his life. Not by a long way.

A short while later, back in the house, Sheila shooed them outside.

'Why don't you and Daniel go for a walk, Colleen? Harry will be fine with me.'

Before Colleen could object, Daniel had taken her by the elbow and steered her outside.

'We'll be back shortly,' he said.

'Where would you like to go?' Colleen asked when they were outside.

'Why don't you show me around? I've never been on a working brood farm before.'

'Okay. If you like. By the way, have you seen Ciaran?'

'Ciaran?' Daniel asked with a frown.

'Yes, Ciaran. The same Ciaran who came to London.'

Daniel stopped abruptly and looked down at her with the strangest expression on his face. 'I want to ask you something,' he said.

'Sure. Although I don't promise that I can answer it.'

Daniel looked around. 'Is there anywhere more private?' he asked. 'Maybe on the other side of the house? Where no one can overhear us?'

'There's a bench down by the lake, but what is it, Daniel? Is there something wrong?'

'Let's go down there and then we can talk.'

Was he going to tell her that her services were no longer needed? That Harry was making such good progress that they could manage on their own? The thought filled her with dismay. She couldn't bear the thought of leaving them, but the truth was that Daniel only saw her as his son's nurse. Oh, she'd no doubt Daniel needed her and liked having her around, but one day soon he and Harry would no longer need her. Harry was making so much progress and his relationship with his father was improving day by day. Which was brilliant. Everything she'd hoped for. Why, then, did it feel as if her heart was been slowly ripped into tiny pieces?

She led the way down a slope at the back of the house until they came to a bench built of stones. Her father had made it when he and her mother had first moved to the farm. He'd always said it was the place he came to when he needed to work out a problem. They sat down next to each other and Colleen was acutely conscious of Daniel's thigh touching hers. She longed to rest her head against him and let the world carry on without them— keep everything the way it was—even for a short while.

'Okay, shoot. Ask me your question,' Colleen said, pushing the thought away. She still had a job to do.

'How many times have you been in love?'

The question took her so much by surprise that she laughed out loud. 'I can't see that that is any of your business,' she said. 'When I said you could ask me anything, I thought it was about Harry. My private life is—private.'

'But you know everything about my private life. Come on, Colleen, we're friends, aren't we?'

Friends? Is that what they were? 'I guess so,' she said slowly. 'Still doesn't mean you can ask me personal questions.'

'Just humour me, please.'

'How many times have I been in love? I had a crush on a boy in my class when I was eight that lasted about a year, but I don't think that counts. Then with Ciaran, I guess.'

'So how did you know that you were in love?'

Colleen laughed again, but it sounded forced, even to her own ears. 'Let me get this right. I'm here because you're looking for some kind of agony aunt. You've met someone and don't know whether it's the real McCoy, is that it?'

Who? Who had he met? When did he have time to be with a woman? As far as she knew, when he wasn't working he was with Harry—or her.

'No. I would know.'

'And how would you know?'

'Because being with that person makes me happy. I want to be with her all the time, want to see her smile, want to make her laugh, want to comfort her when she's down, want to make love to her all the time.' Something in his tone, as if he found the words difficult to say, made her realise he was deadly serious.

'The way you felt about Eleanor when you first got together?' she asked. Envy ate into her soul. It would be something to be loved by Daniel.

'No, the way I felt about Eleanor was different. I wanted her—I thought she was beautiful. But...there was something missing. I only realised that for sure when...' He cleared his throat. 'I only realised that later.'

Colleen's heart was racing. 'I'm not sure where this is going, Daniel.'

He turned so he was facing her. He pushed her hair off her face and, gently cupping his hands on either side of her neck, drew her towards him.

She was frozen to the spot as he brought her lips down on hers, so lightly at first it was almost as if she were imagining it. Then the pressure grew firmer and before she knew what she was doing, her fists were knotting into the front of his shirt as she tugged him closer to her. He groaned and pulled her to her feet, pressing her body into his. She felt as if she were on fire from the tips of her toes to the skin on her scalp. It was as if her body had a mind of its own. She wrapped her arms around him, wanting his kisses to be deeper, moulding her body to the length of his. The world receded as she was sucked into a vortex of desire. His hands dropped to cup her bottom and as he pressed her into him, she felt the unmistakable proof of his desire. She moaned as an answering red-hot flame of desire shot through her pelvis.

She'd never felt like this before. She wanted to rip his clothes from his body, so she could feel his naked skin on hers. She wanted her body to melt into his. She had never wanted anything more in the world.

Suddenly he stopped kissing her and stepped back. She felt bereft and chilled with the sudden loss of his warmth. They were both breathing heavily.

'Did Ciaran ever kiss you like that?' Daniel said hoarsely. 'Did he make you want him so much you can hardly bear it? Did he fill your waking thoughts, your dreams?'

No, was the answer. *Not ever.* Thoughts clambered around her head. But why was he talking about Ciaran?

'Did Ciaran ever love you the way you deserve to be loved? Have you ever responded to him the way you responded just now?' Daniel continued.

'What's Ciaran got to do with anything?' she asked, totally bewildered.

'I need to know if you still love him.'

Colleen gave a shaky laugh. 'Of course I don't. I wouldn't have ended our engagement if I had.'

'So you broke it off?' The look of relief on Daniel's face made her smile.

'Yes,' she said, softly. 'I thought you knew.'

'I needed to be sure. I need to know that there is nothing to stop us being together.'

Her heart was beating so hard, she could hardly breathe. Daniel wanted her.

'Don't you see?' Daniel said triumphantly. 'We can be a family. You, me and Harry.'

His words tore her apart.

She understood now. It had happened before, of course, with other family members of patients she had nursed. He was mistaking gratitude for love. And she well knew those feelings would fade; when Harry no longer needed her, Daniel wouldn't either.

Her arms dropped to her side. 'Daniel, I...'

He seemed oblivious to the change in her.

'Don't you see, Colleen? You belong with Harry and me. You love Harry and perhaps you could love me, too?'

So he'd kissed her so he wouldn't lose her as Harry's nurse? The thought made her feel ill. The arrogance of the man! Did he honestly think one kiss from him was all it took? He couldn't even pretend he was in love with her!

'And of course you know so much about love—with your own failed relationships behind you—your son and your wife for starters.' She couldn't stop herself from lashing out. She was hurting so much inside she thought she'd break apart. 'I'm an employee, so that makes me fair game, does it? Well, let me tell you, if it wasn't for Harry I'd tell you where to shove your job.' Then, before she could say something she was bound to regret later, she turned her back on him and ran back up the slope towards the safety of the house.

She'd only got a little way up the hill before she felt a hand on her arm and she was yanked around to face Daniel.

'Good God, woman. You don't believe that I kissed you because of some crack-minded idea of keeping you as an unpaid nurse? Don't you understand? I'm crazy about you.'

She looked up at him. His green eyes were blazing with such passion she knew he believed what he was saying.

'Oh, Daniel. Maybe you do think you care about me. But it's all really about Harry. People often develop feelings for the people who care for them or their families. But it will pass. I promise you. I'll leave and shortly afterwards you'll forget all about me. That's the way it is.'

He took her by the shoulders and she knew by the way his fingers pressed into her that he was having a hard time not shaking her.

'You're wrong. I will never stop loving you—never.'

She reached up and touched him gently on the cheek. 'You believe that…but in time…' Her throat felt thick and she knew tears weren't far away. She pushed his hands away. 'Let me go, Daniel. Just let me go.'

He had made a mess of that. What had he been thinking? That Colleen would realise as soon as he kissed her that the man she should love was standing right in front of her?

The trouble was he hadn't been thinking. At least not with his head. Weeks of having Colleen around and not being able to touch her, listening to her plans about getting married, had been bad enough when he thought that she was in love with Ciaran and he with her. He shouldn't have rushed her. He should have taken his time, made his feelings clear, but instead he'd waded in and kissed her. He simply couldn't help himself. The truth was he had wanted to kiss her for a long, long time.

And why hadn't he told her that he loved her straight away, instead of clouding the issue with talk of Harry? Good God, a person would think he'd never made love to a woman before.

And there was the rub. He'd made love to plenty of women in the past, more than he could care to name, but he had never been in love before. Not even with Eleanor. Not like this.

So what was he going to do about it?

Not give up. That was for sure. Colleen and he belonged together. She was the missing part of his soul.

All he had to do now was make her believe that.

Colleen headed away from the house and towards the paddock. She wasn't in a fit state to talk to anyone right now. She had to get herself under control first. She touched her lips where Daniel had kissed her. What had got into him? More importantly, what had got into her? She'd responded to him with unadulterated abandon. And if he hadn't started talking about Harry, it wouldn't have stopped there.

Now she wished she'd thrown common sense to the wind and allowed herself to take—if only for the moment—what he had offered her. At least until he came to the realisation he and Harry no longer needed her. But to even think that way was crazy—nuts. She'd only recently broken off her engagement and wasn't about to charge into another one. Especially with Daniel Frobisher—a man whom she'd known for a few short weeks, but who would only break her heart if she let him.

The realisation that she was too late, that she was already in love with him, stopped her dead in her tracks. How could she have been so blind to all the signs?

The mere sight of Daniel made her feel alive in a way she had never felt before. The slightest brush of Daniel's fingertips against her skin set her nerve endings on fire.

But it wasn't just physical attraction she felt for Daniel. She loved being with him. Even if he wasn't touching her, her body felt electrified in his presence. She loved his intensity, his passion, his dedication to his son—everything about him.

She loved Daniel.

She would always love Daniel.

And he cared about her. But for all the wrong reasons. It could never last. Daniel would realise that in time. When she was gone.

She walked over to the paddock and let her horse, Star, nuzzle her hand. Why couldn't life be simple? Why couldn't you love the person who was right for you? Why couldn't the person you loved, love you back? Why couldn't Daniel love her for herself and not because of Harry?

Why did love have to hurt so much?

Colleen tucked the covers round an exhausted-looking Harry. Despite his tiredness, there was finally a glow to his cheeks. Sitting down beside him, she stroked a lock of his blond hair from his eyes. Apart from his immobility, he looked like any other healthy, young twelve-year-old and her heart ached for him.

'Did you have a good day, Harry?' she asked softly.

Harry grinned. 'The best.' He squinted up at her, 'Your brothers are brilliant fun. Even if they are a bit...'

'Nutty?' Colleen finished his sentence for him and laughed. 'Sure, am I not the only sane one in the family?'

When Harry raised his eyebrow he looked so like his father it made her catch her breath. 'If you say so,' he teased back.

Sheila and Colleen had been helping Harry with his walking practice. He could manage the length of the room by himself now. However, Colleen had warned him not to attempt to try walking without her being there ready to catch him, should he stumble.

Colleen leaned over and kissed Harry's forehead. 'Night, sweetheart. Remember, I'm right next door to you if you need anything during the night, okay?' She stood up.

'Colleen, I want to speak to Dad,' Harry said.

'Then I'll get him for you. Are you ready to tell him about your walking?'

'Yes. But I want to talk to him first. Will you stay with me?'

His green eyes so like his father's were filled with

anxiety. No matter how much she wanted to avoid Daniel, she couldn't resist the entreaty in Harry's voice.

'Of course I will, if you want me to.'

'I'll stay with Harry while you fetch Daniel,' Sheila said.

Colleen ran across to the cottage where Daniel was staying. He was sitting outside, looking pensive. Colleen's heart tumbled. How would she get through the next few weeks seeing him every day, yet knowing she had to keep her distance?

'Harry wants to speak to you,' Colleen said.

Daniel got to his feet. 'I was just coming to see him. It's beautiful here,' Daniel said. 'Maybe I'll buy a house in Ireland. I think Harry would like that, don't you?'

'I think he might.'

'He's going to be all right, isn't he? At last I can finally believe it and it's largely down to you, Colleen. I wish I knew how to thank you.'

'I don't need thanks. Harry would have made it on his own.'

'Perhaps. But not so quickly.'

The breeze whipped her hair across her face and Daniel reached across and tucked a stray lock of hair behind her ear. 'You should always wear your hair loose,' he said. The touch of his fingers on her face made her skin sizzle.

'Let's go and see what Harry wants,' Daniel said. 'Then I need you to listen to what I have to tell you.'

His words and the look in his eyes held a promise that made her heart do a complicated routine inside her chest.

Inside Harry's room, Harry was waiting in the chair beside his bed with the sleeping puppy on his lap.

'Hello, Dad,' Harry said.

Daniel ruffled his hair. 'Did you have a good day?'

'Yes. I like it here. Can we stay longer?'

Daniel hesitated and glanced over to Colleen. 'I don't know, son. Colleen's family has their own lives to be getting on with.'

'Of course we can stay for a few more days, if that's what you want, Harry. If your dad doesn't mind. He can always go back to London to finish off whatever he needs to, but you and I can stay here until he comes back. Then you both can stay until his leave is up.'

Harry's eyes lit up. 'Can we, Dad? Then Patch will be old enough for us to take home.'

'If Colleen and her family are up for it, then yes.' Daniel sat down on the bed. 'Is that what you wanted to talk to me about?'

Harry flicked a glance in Colleen's direction. 'Something else,' he mumbled.

'Fire away. You know you can talk to me about anything.'

Something in Harry's expression made Colleen's breath catch in her throat. But she had promised to stay and stay she would. She took the remaining seat beside Harry. Harry was looking at his father. Unshed tears trembled on his long lashes.

'Why did you wait to tell me you were my dad?'

Immediately Daniel was off his feet and crouching by his son's side.

'I didn't know, son. Your mum only told me you were mine and not David's after he left you both. If I'd known, I'd never have let you go. I think your mum knew that. So that's why she didn't tell me.'

Doubt clouded Harry's eyes.

'I didn't tell you this before because I didn't want you

to blame your mother. Once I knew you were mine, I thought the important thing was for us to get to know each other.'

'Mum said you didn't want me. She said you were too busy. And you were.'

'People say things when they're hurt, son.' Daniel continued. 'I hurt your mother. And I'm sorry about that. But she was wrong. I do want you. I love you more than I can say. I'm sorry that I missed you growing up and I'm sorry that I wasn't around for you as much as I should have been. But I'm going to spend the rest of my life making it up to you.'

Harry smiled and Colleen's heart splintered. He looked so much like his father. But that wasn't the only reason her heart felt as if it would shatter into a thousand pieces. Her work with Harry was almost done. All too soon they'd be out of her life and she out of theirs.

'Does that mean you'll buy me whatever I want?' Harry asked. 'Cool.'

Daniel laughed, too. 'What it means is that I promise from now on to put you before my work. No more working at weekends—and we're going to spend every holiday together. You can even choose where we go. You don't even have to go back to boarding school if you don't want to. We can find another school closer that you can attend as a day boy if you like.'

'Hey, Dad. Not so fast. I like my school. All my friends are there. I don't want to spend the rest of my life hanging around with my father—even if he's kind of cool.'

Daniel's eyebrows shot up. 'You think I'm cool?'

'Sort of. For an old man.'

Daniel laughed again. 'Less of the old man, son.'

Harry looked towards Colleen.

'I think there's something else Harry wants you to know, Daniel,' Colleen said, rising to her feet. 'Why don't you go and stand by the door?' Looking baffled, Daniel did as he was asked. 'Are you ready, Harry?' Colleen said softly.

Harry nodded and she helped him to his feet. He swayed slightly as he found his balance. Then she let him go and Harry took one step and then another. Daniel stared at his son and moved forwards as if to help him. Harry stopped. 'No, Dad. I can do it.'

And then, with Harry taking one unsteady step at a time, he walked towards his father and into his arms.

Colleen watched with a lump in her throat as Daniel held his son in his arms. 'I'll leave you two to it, then,' she said. 'I've got to go and see to the horses we had out today—make sure they've got fresh bedding and feed.'

Daniel helped his son on to the bed and lay down beside him, gathering him close.

Colleen closed the door gently behind her, pausing only to look at Daniel lying alongside his son, his arm round his shoulders and the pair of them looking so comfortable together. She felt as if her heart was breaking. She would miss Harry terribly when it came time for her to leave. And as for Daniel? The thought of a life without him was almost too much to bear.

But did she have to live without him?

Love wasn't slow and gentle. Love wasn't boring. At least not with Daniel. It was exciting and unpredictable. It made your legs feel like jelly and your heart sing from a smile. It made you ache in the night from the need to be close. It made the thought of saying good bye unbearable. Colleen had always played it safe. Maybe now it was time to take a chance? Maybe it was time to be rocked out of her safe world? One thing was for sure—it would be a terrifying ride. But also exhilarating. Maybe Daniel did only love her because he felt indebted to her, but she would never know for sure unless she took the risk of finding out.

Happiness washed over her. Maybe Daniel did love her. In the meantime, she would take whatever he had to offer, no matter how short-lived it was.

Daniel eased his arm out from under Harry's shoulders carefully, lest he wake him. Slowly and as quietly as possible, he removed the game console from Harry's lap and, stretching his arm above his head, shuffled off the end of the bed. A floorboard creaked beneath his feet and he held his breath, but Harry didn't move. He was definitely sound asleep.

Reaching for the lamp switch, Daniel hesitated, looking down at his son. He'd always loved him—but never more so than at this very moment. Very gently he stroked a finger down his cheek and in his sleep, Harry smiled.

Daniel could hear the sounds of a game show on the TV coming from the living room. Obviously the family relaxing at the end of a tiring day. He popped his head around the door. Colleen's brothers were all there as well as Sheila.

'If you're looking for Colleen,' Eugene said, 'she's mucking out down at the stables. But if you're looking for company, you're welcome to join us.'

'It's a beautiful evening,' Daniel replied. 'I think I'll go for a walk.' He had to find Colleen. The sky was streaking orange and gold, casting a shimmering light over the lake that was glass still. Was he becoming a romantic? Daniel grinned wryly. So much was changing, himself included, he wouldn't be surprised.

Crunching down the path, he made his way to the stables, wondering if he'd find her still there. But a quick glance in each of the boxes showed resting horses and no sign of Colleen.

He was about to turn on his heel when he noticed a light shining in the barn.

As if sensing his presence, she turned around, showering hay over her shoulder.

'Come to help?' she asked.

'Sure. What would you like me to do?'

Colleen handed him a shovel and pointed to a pile of horse manure. 'Shovel that up for a start.'

Great. Only his love for her could make him touch the stuff. 'Shouldn't your brothers be helping with this?' He knew he was prevaricating, but he was unaccountably nervous. He had to make Colleen believe that what he felt for her had nothing to do with Harry.

'They offered.' Colleen rubbed a hand across her forehead. 'But I love getting back to the farm and mucking in. It keeps me sane.'

Her fingers brushed his and Daniel felt an overwhelming urge to wrap his hand round hers. With her hair tumbling loose from her scrunchie, jeans low on her hips and the porcelain smoothness of her skin, he'd never felt such desire for a woman. Especially one with smudges of dirt on her cheeks and eyes sparking—not with make-up but with fire and laughter. In which case it was better, if he couldn't convince her that he loved her, that soon she'd be leaving him and Harry. He couldn't spend many more days with her and not touch her.

She smiled at him, the moonlight reflecting on her hair turning it to gold.

Daniel removed a piece of straw from her hair and tossed it to the ground. 'That's better,' he said.

She moved towards him and stood on her tiptoes. Her perfume flooded his nostrils, making his head reel. He felt her hands in his hair. 'You have one, too,' she laughed.

He couldn't stop himself. His hands dropped to her waist and his mouth was on hers. He tasted her lips, tentatively at first and then, as she responded, he tugged at the belt of her jeans and pulled her against him.

When she moaned he deepened his kiss. Her tongue flicked against his teeth, driving him crazy with desire. It took all his will-power to pull away from her.

Her eyes were shining and her breath was coming in short gasps.

'God, I want you, Colleen,' he murmured. 'I've wanted you since the first time I saw you. I want to make love to you—badly. But I want you to be sure.'

Her answer was to pull his head back down so his mouth covered hers once more. 'You great lummox, can't you see how sure I am?'

When he released her, she grabbed a horse blanket from one of the stalls and took him by the hand and led him up a ladder into the hay loft. 'Give me your shirt,' she demanded.

He slipped it over his head and passed it to her. She placed the blanket with his T-shirt on top of it and lay down, grinning up at him. She held her arms out. 'Don't you know better than to keep a girl waiting?' she asked.

Later, much later, they lay together. Her head was on his chest, their naked bodies entwined. Rain thudded against the tin roof of the stables like a million bullets. One of the horses stamped his feet and snickered. Colleen called out to the horse and it settled down. She had never felt so peaceful.

'I love you, Colleen.' His voice came out of the darkness. 'I never thought I could love a woman the way I love you.' He put his hands around her waist and swung her around until she was sitting astride him. 'Do you believe me now?'

She grinned down at him. 'Now you wouldn't just be saying that because you've had your wicked way with me, would you?'

'Don't you think I would have said it before I had my wicked way with you? Isn't that the way it's supposed to work?'

She feigned dismay. 'Oops, I got it wrong. Damn.' She felt as if she was floating somewhere above herself.

'So will you stay with Harry and me?'

Some of the happiness dropped out of her world. 'Because of Harry?'

'No, you idiot. Not because of Harry. Because I love you and want to spend the rest of my life with you.' He raked a hand through his hair. 'I didn't think I'd ever say that again. But, yes, Harry is part of the deal. I meant what I said to him earlier. I've got a lot of making up to do. He needs a father.'

'And a mother?'

'Do you think that's why I'm asking? Harry loves you. I love you. I want you in our lives—permanently. I want you to marry me, Colleen. But if you need time, I want you to be with me any way you choose.'

Colleen's heart was singing. 'And here's me just unengaged. Now you're wanting me to do it all over again.'

'The difference is that I want you to do it all over

again, but this time with me. Only me. Only ever me.'
His eyes glinted in the dark. 'I'm warning you, Colleen,
now that I've found you, I don't intend to let you go.'

EPILOGUE

COLLEEN walked up the aisle on Eugene's arm to where Daniel was waiting for her with Harry standing by his side. The last three months had flown by. Harry had continued to improve so much that he was able to walk reasonable distances on his own. His speech was clearer and, although his concentration was less than perfect at times, they were all confident that, with a bit of extra support, he'd be able to resume his studies where he had left off when he returned to school.

In the pews her friends and family smiled at her. Trish, who was her bridesmaid, was grinning from ear to ear as if getting Daniel and Colleen together had been all her doing. Jake from the unit and Kiera were also there, as was most of the staff from the unit in Dublin. Dora was using her handkerchief to dab at her eyes and even Burton's eyes looked suspiciously wet. Colleen and Daniel were going to fund another special unit for brain-injured patients in Dorset and Colleen was looking forward to getting stuck in to the planning of the unit. As she approached the altar, two pairs of shockingly green eyes turned in her direction.

Daniel held out his hand.

She stood next to him as the final strains of the wedding march faded away and knew that life was going to be a roller coaster, but one she intended to enjoy for every breathtaking minute it lasted.

* * * * *

Mills & Boon® Hardback
March 2012

ROMANCE

Roccanti's Marriage Revenge	Lynne Graham
The Devil and Miss Jones	Kate Walker
Sheikh Without a Heart	Sandra Marton
Savas's Wildcat	Anne McAllister
The Argentinian's Solace	Susan Stephens
A Wicked Persuasion	Catherine George
Girl on a Diamond Pedestal	Maisey Yates
The Theotokis Inheritance	Susanne James
The Good, the Bad and the Wild	Heidi Rice
The Ex Who Hired Her	Kate Hardy
A Bride for the Island Prince	Rebecca Winters
Pregnant with the Prince's Child	Raye Morgan
The Nanny and the Boss's Twins	Barbara McMahon
Once a Cowboy...	Patricia Thayer
Mr Right at the Wrong Time	Nikki Logan
When Chocolate Is Not Enough...	Nina Harrington
Sydney Harbour Hospital: Luca's Bad Girl	Amy Andrews
Falling for the Sheikh She Shouldn't	Fiona McArthur

HISTORICAL

Untamed Rogue, Scandalous Mistress	Bronwyn Scott
Honourable Doctor, Improper Arrangement	Mary Nichols
The Earl Plays With Fire	Isabelle Goddard
His Border Bride	Blythe Gifford

MEDICAL

Dr Cinderella's Midnight Fling	Kate Hardy
Brought Together by Baby	Margaret McDonagh
The Firebrand Who Unlocked His Heart	Anne Fraser
One Month to Become a Mum	Louisa George

0212 GEN STD HB

Mills & Boon® Large Print
March 2012

ROMANCE

The Power of Vasilii	Penny Jordan
The Real Rio D'Aquila	Sandra Marton
A Shameful Consequence	Carol Marinelli
A Dangerous Infatuation	Chantelle Shaw
How a Cowboy Stole Her Heart	Donna Alward
Tall, Dark, Texas Ranger	Patricia Thayer
The Boy is Back in Town	Nina Harrington
Just An Ordinary Girl?	Jackie Braun

HISTORICAL

The Lady Gambles	Carole Mortimer
Lady Rosabella's Ruse	Ann Lethbridge
The Viscount's Scandalous Return	Anne Ashley
The Viking's Touch	Joanna Fulford

MEDICAL

Cort Mason – Dr Delectable	Carol Marinelli
Survival Guide to Dating Your Boss	Fiona McArthur
Return of the Maverick	Sue MacKay
It Started with a Pregnancy	Scarlet Wilson
Italian Doctor, No Strings Attached	Kate Hardy
Miracle Times Two	Josie Metcalfe

Mills & Boon® Hardback
April 2012

ROMANCE

A Deal at the Altar	Lynne Graham
Return of the Moralis Wife	Jacqueline Baird
Gianni's Pride	Kim Lawrence
Undone by his Touch	Annie West
The Legend of de Marco	Abby Green
Stepping out of the Shadows	Robyn Donald
Deserving of his Diamonds?	Melanie Milburne
Girl Behind the Scandalous Reputation	Michelle Conder
Redemption of a Hollywood Starlet	Kimberly Lang
Cracking the Dating Code	Kelly Hunter
The Cattle King's Bride	Margaret Way
Inherited: Expectant Cinderella	Myrna Mackenzie
The Man Who Saw Her Beauty	Michelle Douglas
The Last Real Cowboy	Donna Alward
New York's Finest Rebel	Trish Wylie
The Fiancée Fiasco	Jackie Braun
Sydney Harbour Hospital: Tom's Redemption	Fiona Lowe
Summer With A French Surgeon	Margaret Barker

HISTORICAL

Dangerous Lord, Innocent Governess	Christine Merrill
Captured for the Captain's Pleasure	Ann Lethbridge
Brushed by Scandal	Gail Whitiker
Lord Libertine	Gail Ranstrom

MEDICAL

Georgie's Big Greek Wedding?	Emily Forbes
The Nurse's Not-So-Secret Scandal	Wendy S. Marcus
Dr Right All Along	Joanna Neil
Doctor on Her Doorstep	Annie Claydon

0312 GEN STD HB

Mills & Boon® Large Print
April 2012

ROMANCE

Jewel in His Crown — Lynne Graham
The Man Every Woman Wants — Miranda Lee
Once a Ferrara Wife... — Sarah Morgan
Not Fit for a King? — Jane Porter
Snowbound with Her Hero — Rebecca Winters
Flirting with Italian — Liz Fielding
Firefighter Under the Mistletoe — Melissa McClone
The Tycoon Who Healed Her Heart — Melissa James

HISTORICAL

The Lady Forfeits — Carole Mortimer
Valiant Soldier, Beautiful Enemy — Diane Gaston
Winning the War Hero's Heart — Mary Nichols
Hostage Bride — Anne Herries

MEDICAL

Breaking Her No-Dates Rule — Emily Forbes
Waking Up With Dr Off-Limits — Amy Andrews
Tempted by Dr Daisy — Caroline Anderson
The Fiancée He Can't Forget — Caroline Anderson
A Cotswold Christmas Bride — Joanna Neil
All She Wants For Christmas — Annie Claydon